Michael Blake, on his way up in the newspaper profession."

To Amanda, he did seem young to have progressed far in his career, but then he said with a twisted grin, "Of course, it hasn't hurt that my uncle owns the paper. But remember the name. You'll be hearing it often enough from now on. Actually, I've got my eye on TV. That's where the real money is."

In spite of his bantering manner, there was something a little frightening about this young, very ambitious man with his purposeful manner and unmistakable drive. She hoped that the time would never come when . . .

What she had hoped would never happen evidently already had. Michael Blake said, "What's the scam about Solange Bonheur? What were you and the guy you were with looking for in the microfilm room?"

When she turned her head and looked at him, startled, he explained. "I asked Carol — you know, that redhead — who you were and what you wanted, and she told me."

Amanda cried indignantly, "She had no right! I thought that people in a position like hers had some ethics, some code of honor, and could be counted on to keep their mouths shut."

"You're thinking of doctors and lawyers or some such like that," he said calmly. "All of us on *The Messenger* are newspaper people. If there's a story anywhere around we can smell it. Sure we got ethics — loyalty to the firm that pays us. Outside of that, forget it."

He smiled down at her, and she was forced to

admit to herself that he had a charming smile which, she was sure, stood him in good stead when he was coaxing information from an unwilling source. His eyes were a different matter. There was a keen, waiting look in them.

"Meanwhile, back at the obit column . . ."

She turned away quickly, her lips pressed together. Certainly she was not going to tell him what she and Rick had been trying to find out — if Madame Bonheur was truly dead and had been for more than a year.

"So you won't talk, eh?"

He made his voice sound mockingly sinister, and his smile changed to a threatening frown. But he was in earnest. Amanda did not attempt to delude herself about that. She could sense that this was a persistent man. He would not rest until he had all the information he needed and wanted.

He waited only until they reached the walk leading up to the front steps, and then he said, "It's something to do with the fact that Madame Bonheur's will is going to be read in a couple of days, isn't it? That's the reason for the gathering of the clan? Am I right?"

"Roger Platt told you!" she said, annoyed.

"Honey, the probation of a will is a public matter. Notices appear in the newspapers. But you've given me a source. Platt's the lawyer in the case? Thanks!"

Once again she thought that he would not rest until he had found out everything there was to know. He would question everyone who would consent to talk to him. And if he managed to get Matilde to speak to him . . .

Amanda could see the headlines in her imagination:

Dead Woman Reappears to Legatee
Ghost Haunts Old Bonheur Mansion

Things grew even worse. He asked in a voice that might have sounded casual if she hadn't known better, "And what about this granddaughter who gets a mention in the obit? Whereabouts unknown. What happened to Carla Bonheur? Has anybody seen her? Has she shown up anywhere?"

Amanda faltered. "I don't know. She just — she just left, as she had a right to do. She was almost seventeen, after all."

"I remember it vaguely," he told her. "There wasn't much of a to-do about it, was there? Back then, eight years ago, there were droves of kids leaving home. Like an epidemic or something, It's kind of died down, you don't hear so much now about runaways and flower children, like that. Most of them, I guess, came back and maybe even settled down. But the Bonheur girl's never been seen in these parts, has she?"

Amanda wanted desperately to be away from him. She was afraid she might blurt out something she did not want to say. She thought that perhaps if she appealed to him, asked him to forget that she and Rick had ever been in the office of *The Messenger*, he would turn his attention to something else.

She moved closer to him and rested her hand lightly on his arm.

"Michael — "

And at that moment, Rick came around from the other side of the house.

She saw the expression on his face change. He looked puzzled at first, and then, evidently recognizing Michael Blake, tight with suspicion. The two men glared at each other steadily, while she stammered about their having met before in the office of the newspaper.

"While we were looking at the microfilm. You remember, Rick."

The antipathy between them was all too evident in the hard glances they exchanged, a brief growl from Michael, and the crackling of Rick's voice.

"Why are you here? What do you want, Blake?"

"I've already told the young lady. I'm here for a story and in one way or another, I intend to get it."

"But not from us. I might point out to you," Rick snapped, "that you are trespassing. I would not like to get tough about this, but I'll have you removed if you don't get out of here quickly and quietly."

That sort of talk was so foreign to Rick's nature that Amanda could do nothing except stare mutely at him. She was annoyed, of course, by the prospect of newspaper publicity, but she wondered if there might not be another reason for Rick's testiness. A touch of jealousy, perhaps, at finding her in what looked like a friendly situation with a very attractive young man.

He turned abruptly and strode up the steps and into the house. Amanda ran after him, calling his name. He stopped at the foot of the staircase, scowling as he waited for her to join him.

She was surprised when he apologized. "I didn't mean to break up anything. I suppose it's a king-size bore for you, too, with nothing to do. I guess you're entitled to have a date. The only thing is" — he shrugged — "I'm not crazy about the idea of your going out with a newspaper reporter — a young, gung-ho one at that. He might mean trouble for us."

Amanda laughed. "Trouble, we've got. And I don't intend that Mr. Michael Blake, regardless of all his charm, will get one single thing out of me that will do him the least bit of good. And you're wrong on another count. He is *not* my date and never will be."

Rick looked unconvinced for a moment or two. "I suppose it isn't my business anyway. I have no right to pick your friends for you.

"You wouldn't go out with anybody who — "

"There was no 'going out' with Michael Blake," Amanda said definitely. "As for being bored, how could anyone be bored with all the crazy things that go on around here?"

"Always at night," he reminded her. "Just being in this house could space you out. That's why I had to get away from here for a while, just take a walk, sit, and look at the water. This place!"

Her eyes followed his as he looked in the direction of the staircase at the end of the hall. She felt the familiar uneasiness as the gloom of the house seemed to wrap itself around her.

"Can you picture what it would be like to spend your whole life in this place?" Rick asked, sounding more friendly, and as though Michael

Blake had fled from his mind. "It's like somebody had set out on purpose to make it the eeriest place anywhere. So it's back to square one. Got any ideas of what we should be doing now?"

"Taking another look at the music room."

She spoke impulsively, and his eyebrows went up. "You know of anything specific?"

"Well, for one thing, the sheet music has been rearranged."

She told him how she had been in the room a short time ago and of her strange feeling that there was something different there, something she could not describe or put a finger on; finding the restacked sheet music had borne out her feeling.

"Come on, let's give it another look."

He took her arm and led her across the hall. The door of the music room was open, and she could look into it. The dimness was like fog, and the furniture and larger musical instruments appeared ugly.

They began to move around the room, looking at the pieces of sheet music that were stacked in short piles on the surfaces of tables, the piano, even on chairs.

She studied each one with mounting bewilderment and then turned to Rick and whispered, "What does it mean?"

8.

SHE was referring to the titles of the sheet music on the top of each pile. One had, in addition to the title, a picture of an enormous shamrock forming the background for a pretty girl in an Irish costume: "I Will Take You Home Again, Kathleen."

Sometime in the past Amanda had heard someone play and sing that song, and when she opened it to the second page, she recognized the words. She could not remember whether she had heard it in this house or somewhere else. It did not seem as though Madame's guests — the few with whom Amanda had become acquainted — were the type to stand around a piano and sing Irish ballads.

Propped up on the piano's music rack was another sheet of music, this one yellow with age: "Come Back to Erin, Mavourneen."

Amanda turned to Rick and asked, "Why would anyone so devoted to her native country, which in this case was France, have this fondness for the music of some other place? What was it with Madame and Ireland? What was the tie?"

"I'm not convinced there was one. I mean, it could just have happened that those two songs were the only ones of that kind."

He picked up a sheet of music from the flat surface of the slatted graphophone cabinet. He looked at it for a long moment and then shook his head.

"There are others around that don't have anything to do with Ireland. Here." He handed her the sheet of music he had been holding, reached over to take another one from the piano stool, and gave that, also, to Amanda. She read the titles slowly.

"Home on the Range" and "Home, Sweet Home."

Rich asked, "Those mean anything to you?"

"Not a thing, only that they both have 'home' in their titles. And that these pieces weren't in conspicuous places before. Are there any more like these? Let's see if we can figure out what it all means."

They moved around the room, looking at song titles. On a chair near the door, Rick found one that he seemed to think was significant. Its title page showed a road with a cottage at the end of it. Amanda read aloud, slowly: "You're a Million Miles from Nowhere When You're One Little Mile from Home."

"They sure were sloppy in those days," Rick commented. "Can you imagine how that would sound with a rock beat? These must have been meant for human voices only, a catch in the throat sort of thing."

Amanda refused to be diverted. "It's like someone was forming a pattern. But what could Kathleen Mavourneen have to do with a cowboy whose home is on the range? And then this music suddenly appearing. I'm sure there was none of this music out when we were in here the last time."

"What you're telling me is that you think someone came in here and maybe for want of something else to do, moved this stuff around?" he demanded. "Who? Not Ellen, that's for sure. I know if I went upstairs this minute I'd find her in bed where she's been all day. Are you thinking of Matilde? What would be the point of that — "

He broke off abruptly because the footsteps of the woman whose name he had just mentioned sounded from the end of the hall and then grew louder as she came closer.

Rick went to the door of the music room and called her into it. She was dressed for the street in a dark dress printed with white flowers, beautifully cut in a style that had long gone out of date, a prim felt hat, and spotless white gloves. She carried a basket over her arm, and she showed impatience for being delayed. She refused to step over the threshold.

"If you folks expect supper tonight, it's best that you do not hold me up. I'm late as it is," she said resentfully. "The supermarket is jammed at this time. It was better in the old days when all you had to do was call up the butcher and he'd send up what you needed. You could trust him to do right by you, too. You never got anything you couldn't put on your table. Now who cares — ?"

She broke off her nostalgic yearning for the past and looked grim again, but for a few moments she had been softer, more human than the two young people had ever known her to be. It gave Amanda the courage to ask her a question.

"Who was here in the music room today?"

Matilde immediately became as she usually was: cross and unfriendly. "Back to your mysteries again, Miss? Trying to start trouble when there is none?"

But her eyes slid away, and her voice had dwindled when she cried, "*Mon Dieu*, such foolishment!"

She turned and walked to the entrance door, her back stiff. When she was out of earshot, Amanda asked Rick, "Have you noticed that whenever Matilde is upset or — or afraid, if that's what it is — she used words and phrases in French?"

He did not answer, seeming depressed by yet another failure, and Amanda could not think of anything at all which would raise his spirits. She thought back to the first night she had spent in this house in eight years, beginning with the sound of crying in the tower room.

She cried, "Why have we never tried to find out what was in there? It's only logical. I did hear sounds coming from the tower room. And we never did anything about it. Don't you think we should?"

"It's a pretty sure bet that the door to the place is locked. And that Matilde has the key," he said thoughtfully. "But maybe there's another one somewhere."

"Hanging on a hook near the back door," Amanda remembered. "They were always there. Matilde had hers, of course, but those were duplicates. Come on, let's go and see if we can find them."

They left the music room and hurried down the length of the hall and through the green baize door into the kitchen. There was still the scent of something Matilde had been baking. The geraniums on the windowsill, the copper pots and pans on the walls all looked very cheery, and it was hard to imagine that this place harbored evil and danger under its roof.

Rick muttered, "All it needs is a calico cat purring on a rocking chair."

In spite of the coziness of the kitchen Amanda hurried Rick out of it. Excitement was mounting inside her at the prospect of examining the tower room. She thought that if they did not find the key to it, she would break down and cry.

The bunch of keys were there where she had remembered them to be, on a hook near the back door. Rick took them and went through them all until he found the one they were looking for. Attached to it was a small tag on which was printed TOWER 2.

It was an odd shape, unlike the other keys,

which were identified as being those to the front and rear doors, the side entrance, the various bedrooms, and the storage places in the cellar.

They went upstairs and there was a suspenseful moment when Rick inserted the small piece of metal into the keyhole on the tower room door. But nothing happened. As he turned it back and forth, it made no sound, nor did it open the lock. His hand moved impatiently and finally there was a faint squawking sound and he cried, "Got it!"

He put his hand around Amanda's arm, and they went slowly and cautiously into the room together. It was a small, circular place and had a strong odor of disuse. It needed airing out, yet they knew that someone had been in there not very long ago, for on the dusty carpet there were footprints that looked fairly fresh.

At one corner of the room there was a spiral staircase that curved upward. Rick ascended a few steps and then came back to where Amanda was standing.

"Nothing much of importance in here," he said in a disappointed voice. "Not one stick of furniture. Nothing left around that'd give us an idea of whose footsteps they are."

He pointed to the carpet at their feet. "Take a look there, Mandy. Do those look as though they belong to a man or to a woman?"

She studied them carefully and then said, the excitement rising inside her, "There are two sets, aren't there? Look, one set's larger than the other."

All the light in the room came from the windows, which were mere slits high on the wall.

Rick got down on his knees and shook his head. "First prize for stupidity!" he said. "I should have known enough to bring a flashlight."

He went on examining the footsteps for a few minutes and then said, "You're right. I guess there are two people in this mess. Two on the staircase when you were pushed down, two different kinds of shoes here in this room — and that means two people wearing them. Mandy, take another look. Doesn't it seem to you that those small ones are very delicate? I'd say a woman at first glance but it might be a boy. The toes are rounded, which might mean sneakers. Everybody wears them, boys *and* girls. We've got them on right now. So all that means is that there were two people in here not long ago, two people with different-size feet."

Amanda remembered the sound of crying she had heard coming from this room, and she shivered at the memory. The thought of someone in this very place, lurking there, perhaps waiting for her to fall asleep so that she might be awakened by that awful sound, was upsetting.

"Hey, don't let it get to you!" Rick gave her a little shake "Let's split. There's nothing we can do in here anyway. One more strikeout. What do we do next, if anything?"

A moment later he answered his own question. "You don't suppose Ellen was wandering around, do you? Ever notice what small feet she has? Some unreal size like four double A. Why don't we wake her up and ask her if she's been in this room since we've been back here in Lake Falls?"

But when they reached Ellen's bedroom, knocked, and went in, they found it empty.

She did not seem to be anywhere in the house. They started with the rooms downstairs, making quick inspections of the kitchen, dining room, the library, Maurice Bonheur's study, the back parlor. They glanced into the music room, unlocked the cellar door, and called down into the darkness below. There was only the hollow echo of their own voices.

Now Amanda began to feel real fear. She said to Rick as they went back to the front of the house, "It's this dreadful house! It's like something evil got into it and has stayed here all those years. Just a little while ago, I was searching for *you.* I thought you had disappeared. Now it's Ellen. I wish I had never come back here! And if you hadn't come, Ellen wouldn't . . . she wouldn't . . ."

He did not scoff this time, but she was sorry she had blurted out her fear for Ellen. He must be suffering from his own agony, worried about the sister who was so dependent upon him. His face was grim and set, and she pitied him because he did not want to voice his terrors, preferring to keep them locked up inside him.

He, too, must be remembering that eight years ago another girl had vanished from this place and has never been seen again.

They went from room to room, many of them empty, but some of them furnished with old-fashioned articles, which had evidently been well cared for during the years. Rick's face grew grimmer, and his jaw became so tight that it seemed to hurt him to speak.

Amanda suddenly remembered something and cried out, "Where did *you* go?"

He stared at her blankly. "Go?"

"You disappeared for a while, and I went through the same thing searching for you. Then you suddenly appeared —"

"And broke up that little scene with Blake, the super reporter." She tried to speak, but he went on without listening to her. "I went for a walk. I found I couldn't stand this place any longer, had to get away. How about it? That satisfy you?"

"Rick, don't be angry." She placed a hand gently on his sleeve. "I just thought it might help us to find Ellen."

"Sorry!" he growled. "But it's getting to me now. I shouldn't take it out on you. We're in this together, and we've got to stick together."

The afternoon was drawing to a close, and although Rick flicked on light switches when they passed them, the long halls seemed wrapped in gloom.

Matilde Gerard returned with her basket full of food. Amanda had had one little hope that Ellen might have finally decided to get up and go out, and then had met Matilde and had gone shopping with her. It had been a vain hope. Amanda realized that now and told herself that she should have remembered that there was not that much friendliness between Matilde and any of the young people.

They made another trip to the tower room, Rick saying desperately that there must be something there they had overlooked, something that would give them some hint as to who had been in there and left the footprints on the dusty carpet.

They looked at each other in despair. Amanda wished that she could think of something to say to Rick to comfort him and reassure him about his sister. But she needed reassurance herself.

This must be, she thought, one of the darkest days of my life.

9.

SUPPER was a sad, silent affair, Ellen's empty seat robbing Rick and Amanda of their appetite. All the rooms in Chanson were overly large, and sitting at each end of the dining table, the two young people felt miles apart. It was senseless to go on sitting there, Amanda thought, for she could scarcely swallow a bit of food, and she knew that Rick was feeling the same way.

Matilde served them without uttering a word but she was not very adept at hiding what she was thinking. They could sense her annoyance when she removed half-filled plates and was not allowed to replace them with others. But there was more than annoyance; she seemed tense and nervous.

They left her grumbling over the ruined meal and went out onto the porch. The long dusk of late summer was fading into darkness, and the first stars were beginning to appear in the sky. Thoughts of Ellen out there in the coming night, among strangers perhaps, made Amanda's heart beat faster with fear.

"We can't let it go on like this any longer," she said to Rick urgently. "We're going to have to call the police. I think we've waited too long as it is. You know we've got to find her before it gets really dark."

"You know what will happen, don't you? The police get into it and it means a lot of sensational publicity."

"It doesn't matter," she said stubbornly. "Rick, how can you think about things like that when Ellen's gone? We've got to —"

He went on as though she hadn't spoken, "Your friend Michael Blake will be right up there at the head of the pack of news hounds. Can't you see the headlines? I could write them myself. 'Second Mysterious Disappearance from House of Mystery.' The paper's probably got on file pictures of Carla taken years ago and maybe others of Madame, and they'll send a photographer down to snap some of Chanson. Do you want to see those splashed all over the front page?"

"Of course not. But we can't wait much longer. Rick," she said gently, "I know it's hard for you to face the truth. We could go on all night like this, fooling ourselves and each other that Ellen's just taking a walk and will turn up at any minute. But that's unreal. She never goes off alone, does she? And there's the danger . . ."

She had been going to point out the peril that lay at the bottom of the lawn — the water, slate-colored now and gleaming dully. But she could not get the words out.

She could not add to the anguish she saw in his eyes. In spite of his words about publicity and newspapers and their intrusive pictures and stories, she knew he was even more terrified than she.

He and Ellen had always been close. Years ago he had always been patient, even before the accident, with his tagalong little sister, even when he had been doing his own tagging along after Carla Bonheur.

"All right," he conceded at last, "we'll have to have help."

At that moment they both turned at the sound of shrubbery rustling and twigs cracking, and Ellen appeared at the edge of the walk that led to the porch.

Rick rushed down the steps and took her into his arms. He hugged her to him and then, after that brief, relieved embrace, he began to scold her.

"I almost went bananas with worry!" Although his face was stern and reproving, Amanda could see the tenderness in his eyes. "Where have you been all this time?"

She smiled serenely but did not answer him. When he asked the question again, she shrugged and put her hands out, palms up. Amanda had learned that Ellen used certain gestures to express things she could not say. This one seemed meaningless, and Rick was beginning to sound impatient when he said, "Ellen, don't con me. You know what I'm asking. Come on, tell us where you were. Use your pad."

She took out the ballpoint pen and pad from

the pocket of her skirt. She wrote two words, tore off the sheet of paper, and handed it to her brother. "Music Room."

He read them aloud to Amanda. "Now, what's that supposed to mean? We looked in there, didn't we, Amanda? Didn't we search through all the downstairs rooms?"

She nodded. She thought of all the rooms they had looked into, the music room being among them. She knew that if Ellen had been in there, she would have been seen. Unless she had been deliberately hiding.

Had she been playing a game to relieve the boredom of this gloomy old house? But this went beyond mischief, and the last time she had seen Ellen, the girl had been huddled in her bed, in the grip of some sort of malaise.

"Ellen," Amanda asked quietly, "what were you doing in the music room? We've been looking for you for hours. Don't you realize what you put Rick and me through?"

Ellen's eyes had a strange and unreadable expression. It could have been a stubborn hardness, a determination not to reveal anything more than she already had. But then the look softened and became a look of appeal. It seemed that if she could have spoken, she would have pleaded not to be pressed for answers.

"But you must tell us," Rick said firmly, "where you've been."

Ellen wrote quickly on the pad as though this was one question she did not mind answering. "Went for a walk." He looked at the words and then asked, "Alone?"

She nodded. Rick would have persisted further but Amanda intervened. "Let it go for now, Rick. Can't you see she's exhausted?"

The weariness was in the pallor of her face and its drained look. When she smiled her gratitude to Amanda, the sweet, docile look was gone from it. She seemed to be forcing her lips to move. When Amanda asked her if she were hungry, she shook her head forcibly, and she began to edge toward the door as though she were eager to be away from them. Amanda was determined that she would not be. She did not intend to allow Ellen out of her sight that night.

She led Ellen upstairs to her bedroom. She pulled down the window shades and turned on a light while Ellen was undressing and getting in between the sheets.

The room was still warm and almost completely airless. Not even the lightest breeze came in through the open window or fluttered the shades.

"I'll put these up when you're all ready for sleep and I can turn the light off." Amanda spoke softly. "Ellie, dear, you know how Rick and I feel about you. You can imagine how worried we were when you took off to wherever you went this afternoon. Promise me you won't do that again. We'll be going home soon, so let's make the best of it for what time is left."

She felt a little twisting of sadness at the thought of parting with this girl whom she had always loved, and who had grown even dearer to her during the past few days. As for how she would feel at being separated from Rick . . . she turned that thought firmly out of her mind.

But she spoke of him to Ellen. "You upset your brother dreadfully." She went back to the window to raise the shade. "And if there's something you should tell us, anything that you know and we don't, remember we're all in this together —"

She broke off suddenly because the shade seemed to fly out of her hands, and it went racing upward and rolled swiftly around and around on its holder.

Amanda stretched out her hand, but found she could not reach it without standing on something. She muttered, "Darn!" and went to get a chair. Then she looked out through the glass pane and saw something that almost made her lose her balance and fall off the chair.

A man in a sports jacket and light slacks stood, under the shadow of a leafy tree, staring up at the house.

"You're letting this thing knock you off the wall," Rick said when she told him about it. "We've already had that, remember? Can't have the prowler bit twice, can we? Who but your friend Michael Blake would be lurking around in the half-dark? Maybe you knocked him for such a loop that he's hanging around, hoping for a glimpse of your super-lovely face. Perhaps he's even trying to get up his courage to come to the door and ask for a date."

The childish outburst of jealousy might have amused her under other circumstances. It may even have pleased her. But now she was merely annoyed.

"For your information," she said coldly, "it was not Michael that I saw. This man was huskier. And, from what I saw of him, quite a bit older. And not," she added slyly, "not nearly as good-looking. Well, whatever, I'm going down and see if he's still there. If you want to come with me — fine! Otherwise I'll go alone."

"It's crazy," he complained, "but you know I'm not going to let you do a thing like that alone." He suddenly looked at Ellen, as though remembering her presence. She was listening to and watching them with great interest. Rick said to her, "It's nothing, honey. Our friend Amanda just has this power to attract all sorts of lovelorn swains. This one is probably one of them. We'll check him out and be back in a few minutes."

Amanda held to an indignant silence as they went downstairs. She led him over to the tree under which the stranger had been standing. "Here, right about here."

There was no one there or anywhere in sight.

"Of course not," Rick said, disgruntled. "I should have known that it wasn't going to be that easy."

He didn't want to say anything more about the man she had seen or, as he said, thought she had seen. Although Amanda kept insisting that indeed she *had* seen a strange man standing there and staring up at the windows, Rick made it clear that he was not interested.

Instead, he began to make plans for the coming

night. That was a matter that had to be settled right away, he said grimly. The danger seemed to be growing.

He would spend the night downstairs in Maurice Bonheur's study. From that point he would be able to see or hear anything that went on on the first floor. He would wait until everyone in the house was asleep and then sneak downstairs and keep his vigil. He had not decided yet what he would use for a weapon, but she could be sure that he'd have one and use it if necessary.

That was only bravado, Amanda guessed — at least she hoped it was — but she could not be sure. He had given her something new to worry about. She'd heard of people who were unfamiliar with guns doing something horrifying like shooting off their own toes. She wondered uneasily if Maurice Bonheur had kept a gun in the house, and if Rick was aware of its whereabouts.

"You'll call me if you need me," she begged. "Don't do anything unless I'm there."

He gave her a long, thoughtful glance and finally said, "It's a deal. You'll stay close to Ellen, though. Won't you?"

She nodded, and then the long, dark, dreadful night began.

10.

SHE awoke to the sound of the music. At first she did not remember where she was. Her mind groped, and then she knew. Early in the evening, she had taken her pillow and a blanket into Ellen's room and settled into an easy chair, determined that she would not fall asleep. She had intended to spend the entire night there, remaining awake to hear any sounds that might break the dense silence.

She had left the door open to the hall and a light burning out there. She had expected that Ellen would be curious as to why she had a guest in her bedroom, but she merely smiled and nodded when Amanda told her that she would be sitting up in the chair all night. The expected question on Ellen's pad did not materialize. There was merely docile acceptance. Sleep came to Ellen quickly. It was as though she was glad to escape into oblivion.

Amanda, who had been determined to remain awake, dozed for a while and then sank into a deep sleep.

The music came from downstairs, a whining, sad sort of sound. Amanda did not know how long it had been going on before she became aware of it. Actually, it seemed to be part of a dream she had been having, but now that she was fully conscious she drew a long, shuddering breath. This was the same type of music she had heard before, but somehow it seemed louder and sadder now.

Amanda threw aside the blanket and got to her feet. She was halfway to the door, moving quietly in order not to awaken Ellen, when the music stopped. It was then that she smelled the perfume.

There could be no mistake about it. Madame Bonheur had invariably worn a light scent of violets. The scent was now so strong that she choked a little. Madame's room was at the front of the house. It was the only room Amanda and Rick had not inspected when they'd been searching for Ellen. What they thought of as a bedroom was actually a small suite, for there was a sitting room, Madame's own bath, and a dressing room. An old, leftover restriction had kept the two young people from going in there. During the summers they had spent at Chanson, Madame's private quarters had been off limits.

Amanda had had only brief glances of it when its door had been open, and she had a reason for being in that part of the house. She had seen a lacy, dainty bedspread, curtains tied back with lavendar satin ribbons, mirrors in all parts of the bedroom, a dressing table with a stiffly starched skirt, and everywhere Madame's favorite color — pale purple.

Amanda hesitated when she was halfway down the hall. Why didn't Rick come? she wondered. He had said that they were in this together. He was supposed to be in Monsieur Bonheur's study on the first floor. He should have heard the music, been awakened by it if he had been asleep.

She had no wish to go wandering about in this fearsome house alone, especially not now when she thought she saw a flash of movement from down the hall in the direction from which the odor of violets was coming.

"Rick?"

It could not be Rick. There had been something about that movement, which reminded her of Madame in the old days when she had stolen up behind them in order to catch them in mischief. When she did, it had always been Carla who had been the guilty one, but she always had gone unpunished.

Rick came up behind her from the other direction. She heard his footsteps and whirled, a scream stuck in her throat, her heart seeming to have stopped until she saw who it was.

"Were you trying to scare me to death?" she hissed. "You almost did it!"

He said he was sorry and confessed that he had fallen asleep. "When I came to, I heard the music. But it stopped almost right away. I did a stupid thing," he added ruefully. "I found a hunting knife in Monsieur's collection, put it down somewhere, and then couldn't find it. Really great investigator, wouldn't you say? By the time I found it the music had stopped. I finally got to the music room, but there was no one there. There was a funny feeling about the room — I don't know just what it was. The window was open but it didn't seem cold enough to cause the shivers, which is exactly what it did." He shuddered at the memory. "Empty. I took a good look around. There was no one in that room."

He lifted his head and sniffed. "What is that awful smell? It's like someone emptied a quart jar of perfume over everything."

"Madame's violets. Don't you remember?"

"Now that you mention it, sure. But never like this. Never so strong it would knock you over. That's where it's coming from? Down there?" And he peered through the gloom in the direction of the other end of the hall. "What are you doing out of Ellen's room?"

"The same thing you are. Trying to get to the bottom of this mess."

She told him about thinking she had seen someone down past Madame's bedroom door, and he asked, "The phantom again?" Then, as he saw her lips tighten, he added hastily, "Well, you don't sound too sure of what it was you did see. And I can't believe it's helping anything, our hanging around up here like this. Let's go down to the kitchen and get a glass of milk and maybe make some sandwiches."

She said in disbelief, "At a time like this? You can think of food?"

He retorted defensively, "I didn't eat much at supper. And don't forget, I'm still a growing boy.

I came up through the kitchen and the back stairs. And I didn't stop to get anything to eat then." Somehow he had managed to make himself sound undeniably virtuous.

She said, hastily, "All right, growing boy. Don't break down completely. But we'll go down the front way. As I remember, those back stairs are pretty steep and dark."

He took her hand, and they walked to the head of the staircase. She put her hand on the banister and was about to take the first step downward when he suddenly tightened his grip and pulled her back roughly.

She cried out in protest, but then he said, "Look," and she saw that he was pointing at a piece of string stretched across the stairs from one side to the other. It was an ordinary piece of red twine, the kind used by shopkeepers to wrap around boxes and packages, more specifically those that held bakery products.

Amanda stepped backward, clutching the banister. Her voice sounded full of horror as she said, "It was put there so we would trip over it and fall down the stairs! Oh, Rick!"

He was bending down, examining the length of string, touching it gently with one hand, testing its strength.

"No, I don't think so." He drew himself up to a standing position. "I want to take a closer look at this, how it's fastened and things like that. There's a flashlight in my room. I'll be back in a minute."

"You're not leaving me here alone!" she protested. "Not when you know somebody rigged this trap for me while I was asleep."

But he was gone by then; it was only a few minutes later that he returned, his way led by the cone of brightness. He played it on the carpet, swung it from side to side, looked carefully at the places where the string was fastened. The moment he loosened it a little from the thumbtacks that held it, it grew slack.

"As soon as we, or maybe I should say I, got my foot caught in it," Amanda said, shuddering, "I'd go plunging down the stairs, and this time they'd be no one to keep me from being killed."

He disagreed with her. "All that would happen would be that you'd pull the twine out of the wall. There's no chance at all that it would cause a fall. A piece of wire now — that would do the trick. A good taut length of wire fastened with something stronger than thumbtacks. So what was the point of this foolish bit of business? What have I ever done to anybody?"

"Not you," Amanda told him softly. "Unfortunately, you were just an innocent bystander who got involved. It's evidently my party, and you just got caught up in it. Maybe the person who stretched this twine across the steps didn't know it wasn't strong enough or tight enough to do any real damage."

"Then he would have to be a first-class idiot. Mandy, someone is putting on a campaign of scare tactics. None of these things was designed to really hurt you. Except, maybe, the push downstairs, but even then there was somebody to catch you and break your fall. Maybe, after all, you'd better quit. There might be a slipup and all the big bucks in the world wouldn't be much good if you weren't around to spend them.

"I'll tell you one thing," he said, rolling the length of twine around his knuckles, "I'm not going to burst out crying after the will is read."

There was a thoughtful gleam in his eyes as he looked at Amanda. "It doesn't look as though that will is going to bring us much luck, welcome as the money will be. If there is any. What a rotten joke that would be on us if we go through all this hassle, and it turns out that Madame left each of us one of those ugly figurines in the drawing room and nothing else!"

Amanda was busy with thoughts of her own. "It all goes back to the will, doesn't it? Maybe she left something to Matilde, but I'd guess that most of her money goes to us — you and I and Ellen — just the three of us now that Carla is legally dead. If anything should happen to me, everything would be left to you and Ellen."

He turned an astonished look upon her. "Well, thanks! Thanks a lot!"

She tried to convince him that she had not meant that the way it sounded, but she was aware that the thought had come from somewhere, that it had been on her mind. Otherwise she would not have expressed it.

"Richard Stanton, the mad ogre of Chanson Castle," he said in a tight voice. "The phantom of the haunted tower room!"

She could not stop her laughter from bubbling out. "Don't be silly! You know that wasn't what I meant."

"What then?"

She had no honest answer. He was waiting, and she knew that she must explain her statement. She drew a long breath and the smell of violets, still hanging heavily on the air, filled her nostrils.

Rick, too, was conscious of it. "That stuff didn't spray itself around. Maybe we ought to move along the hall and find out just where it's coming from. And why."

He took her hand and led her along the hall until they reached the door that led to Madame's suite. It was open, and at that point the odor was almost overpowering; Amanda hung back at the threshold, groping in her skirt pocket for a handkerchief.

She had never cared for perfume, never using anything except a little light cologne and faintly scented talcum powder. Now this heavy, pervasive smell was making her feel ill.

Giving her a keen look, Rick said, "There's no point in our going through all the rooms. We know where the smell's coming from. But that doesn't tell us anything important."

He turned his flashlight in one bright arc about the room and then moved to the door to close it. There was a faint, crunching sound under his feet. He bent and picked up a sliver of grass from the carpet. There were others shining under the light of his flashlight. He took several of them in his hand and held them to his nose.

"Somebody broke a bottle of this sickening stuff and probably couldn't mop it up. The carpet's too thick for that; the liquid's seeped far into the shag. So, for all the good it does us, we know that much. There was a person in here tonight who had butterfingers."

He was right, of course. There must have been an intruder in Madame's exquisite boudoir. Somehow the room did not seem to be at all charming this time. In the gloom, with only the light from the hall and Rick's torch upon the various furnishings, it had a look of sadness. As all rooms must when those who had occupied them went away forever, Amanda thought.

Rick found other slivers of glass by moving his foot about, but said that they should be left there.

"What good would it do to carry them around? Matilde will probably be in here to clean up in the morning. I wouldn't be surprised if she's in here every day, keeping this place like a shrine."

He drew an unhappy breath. "Now how about that great idea you had about raiding the fridge?"

They both laughed and went downstairs.

The refrigerator was well stocked, and Rick was not a fussy eater, assenting to everything she suggested they put in their sandwiches. Before her amazed eyes, he drank almost an entire quart of milk.

It wasn't until he had finished everything that he spoke of Ellen.

"I suppose we shouldn't have left her up there alone. She was okay, wasn't she, Mandy? Before the music started, I mean. And when you left her there."

She remembered guiltily that she had not given Ellen a thought when she had awakened abruptly, nor later when she had been absorbed with Madame's perfume.

"Oh, I'm sure she's all right."

He did not seem to notice that she had not answered his question. He got up, crumpled his paper napkin and threw it into a wastebasket, and then carried his glass and plate over to the sink.

"Well, I guess we've fooled around long enough. Next stop — music room. Right?"

Amanda breathed a tired, discouraged sigh. "I doubt that we'll find anything there that'll do us any good. If there was anybody in there, he — or she or them — will probably be gone. You'll see. There won't be anybody around."

She was wrong. There was somebody, and it was the last person in the world they would have expected to see coming out of the music room.

11.

THEY had heard the unmistakable sound of someone moving about, the whisper of footsteps, the rustle of silk. Rick had signaled to Amanda to flatten herself against the wall so that she, as well as he, could see anyone coming out of the music room.

For a few minutes, which seemed like hours to Amanda, they stood like that: quiet and unmoving. And then the sounds became louder as the person inside the room came closer to the door. It was Ellen.

Amanda's first thought was that Ellen was sleepwalking. But it fled quickly for she did not have the attitude or the stance of a sleepwalker. Her hands were at her sides and her body was not rigid; she seemed to know exactly where she was and where she was going.

She passed within a few feet of where Rick, and Amanda stood scarcely breathing. But she did not see them, did not even turn her head as she crossed the hall and went up the staircase.

Rick did not move until his sister disappeared into the shadows of the second floor. Then he released the breath he had been holding and said, "We should have grabbed her, shouldn't have let her get away! I was afraid for a few minutes that she was walking in her sleep. She used to once in a while, you know, when she was a little kid. But this wasn't it. Come on, let's go up there now. She's got a lot of explaining to do."

Amanda held him back with a hand around his wrist. "You'll frighten her if you start accusing her."

"Frighten her? After all that's been going on! And don't tell me she hasn't been onto everything. She's not stupid, you know, even if she can't tell us what's in that head of hers."

"I'll grant you that. But, Rick, you've forgotten some of the things that happened. You couldn't be seriously thinking that she could push me down the stairs and arrange to have someone break my fall? Or put that twine across the steps? Or scare me half to death by crying in the tower room."

She thought of something else. "I was asleep when someone went into Madame's room and took her bottle of perfume. But I'd have woken up quickly enough if Ellen had left the room. The breaking of the bottle was an accident, of course. And that just added to the confusion."

"It's hard to believe that Ellen had any part in all those crazy things," Rick said. Maybe it was nothing but mischief. Maybe we don't really know

88

Ellen. Could be there's a different girl inside, one that resents being mute and is trying to get even or, if you won't buy that, is just relieving her boredom."

Amanda, shocked, cried, "You can stop right there. You're talking about Ellen. Somebody else might think and act that way but not that dear little girl. She's so — well, childlike and innocent. Besides, she couldn't be the one who broke the perfume bottle. We would have smelled it when she went by us just now. When the glass broke, the liquid would have splashed on her feet, her ankles. As strong as it was, the smell would have clung to her until she could have taken a shower, and I don't think she did. She wouldn't have had time after we went downstairs. Besides, the hot water heater is faulty. I found that out. If you don't take your bath or shower early in the day, forget it. There's no hot water to be had."

Rich said that he had discovered that also. But he said he's certainly like to know where Ellen had been while they were searching for her. That might be the key to the whole business. Amanda shook her head. There were too many things still unexplained, she argued. Things like who had been in the tower room, where the music had been coming from, who had tied a piece of red twine across the staircase and dropped Madame's perfume bottle. Neither of them mentioned the apparition Amanda had seen on two occasions.

They waited until they heard a bedroom door shut upstairs and agreed it must be that of Ellen's bedroom. Then they started their new investigation in the music room, because that was closest at hand, and their curiosity as to why Ellen had been there at this time of night was too sharp to be ignored.

A window was open, and Amanda was on her way over to it when Rick called her back.

"No one could have gotten into the house that way. That table's in the way, and it looks like solid mahogany. It would take a couple of strong men to move it and we'd have heard anything like that going on."

He was right, of course. The table was long and so sturdy that it could not have been easily moved. There was some sort of old-fashioned instrument upon it and beside that a pile of sheet music.

Amanda changed her direction and walked around the room, looking at other stacks of music which, as far as she could tell, seemed to be in the same order as when she had last seen them. Rick had picked up a guitar and was strumming it lightly.

"Did what we hear sound anything like this to you?" he asked. "I thought an electric guitar perhaps, but there doesn't seem to be one around anywhere." He glanced about and went back to his strumming. "They didn't have them in Madame's day, I guess."

"I'm sure not. But didn't Ellen play an instrument when she was younger? I seem to remember her talking about it."

"The flute. When she was in the third grade, all the kids in her school took lessons on something. They were going to form a band. She did learn to play it some and used to practice in her room.

Then, after what happened here that summer, she never went back to it."

He put the guitar back in the corner where he had found it. Crossing the room, he glanced idly at the piano. The keyboard was closed now. When they had last seen it, it had been open and they had been able to see the keys, now grown a little yellow with age.

There was a slip of paper resting on the cover, and Rick moved closer to it and looked down at it curiously.

"Hey! What do you think this means?"

Amanda went to his side. He picked up the slip of paper and handed it to her. There was only a name printed on it, and that was in heavy block letters: CHARLENE.

"What's that got to do with anything?" Rick wondered. "We've had Kathleen and Mavourneen, and now we've got Charlene. Where does she come into the picture? We didn't find anything along the way with that name, did we?"

A moment later, in a voice grown heavy, he said, "Ellen. That's a piece of paper from her pad, isn't it? Why won't she tell us, Mandy? She probably could help us clear this whole miserable business up if she'd only trust us, confide in us."

Amanda felt her sympathy touched. She tried to think of something to say to console him. "This might not have anything to do with all those things that have happened. Maybe she's just playing a game with us. Don't you remember when we were kids that Ellen and . . . and Carla and I played a treasure game? We invited you to take part, but you were an arrogant little monster. You said that it was kindergarten stuff, like looking for eggs on Easter morning."

She stopped speaking abruptly, for she remembered that there had been an unpleasant ending to that game, which they had played only once. Carla had been the one who had hidden the clues. Ellen and Amanda had been the ones who had done the searching.

Together they had faithfully followed clue after clue, each one cleverly worded to make the search more arduous than amusing. But they finally reached the last one.

The words on the slip of paper read: "I'm old and straight as can be/ Squirrels hide their nuts in me."

They had guessed immediately that the verse described the great tree at one side of the house. There was a large hole halfway up the trunk, and Amanda, who was the taller of the two girls, raised herself on tiptoe and put her hand in the opening in the trunk. Her groping hands found a cardboard box and she drew it out.

While Ellen hovered about excitedly, Amanda opened the box. And then she let it slip out of her hands. The screams of the two girls made a chorus of horror. The box had contained a dead snake, which now lay curled at their feet.

Amanda had forgotten that particular episode and now, as she recounted it to Rick, all the horror came back.

His face looked hard and set by the time she had finished. Was he battling with disillusionment and self-blame for not having recognized Carla's cruelty years ago?

He demanded harshly, "Are you saying that Ellie left that piece of paper there and expects us to guess something from that name? Listen, I've had just enough of this nutty business. Suppose we just let it ride until tomorrow? Then maybe our minds will be fresher; the brains will be working better; we'll be in better all-around shape. I'll coax Ellie a bit and get her to come out with whatever it is she's hiding. Who knows? There may not be one more crazy happening before the will is read."

Did he really believe that? she wondered. Or was he trying to convince himself that life would suddenly be peaceful at Chanson; the danger would miraculously disappear; they would leave Madame Bonheur's house in high spirits and very rich indeed.

"There's the rest of the night to get through," she reminded him. "What harm could there be in asking Ellie a few simple questions now?"

He insisted that this was not the time to do it. They were both tired, their nerves were on edge, each had developed a stubborn streak. They were very close to a quarrel.

She pressed her lips together so that she would not say something she would regret later. She watched Rick walk down the hall to his bedroom, and her spirits fell lower and lower. She had never felt so alone.

12.

"IF you would only tell me something, give me some hint," Amanda pleaded for what seemed like the hundredth time. "Ellie, darling, there's a whole morning and part of the afternoon to get through. That's eight hours. A whole day!"

Amanda had awakened early on this day, the day the will of Solange Bonheur was to be read. She had gone immediately to the window, looked out, and seen nothing except the fog pressing against the glass. The heat wave of the past few days had broken. A chill dampness had seeped into the house — that and an uncomfortable, waiting atmosphere that made Amanda uneasy.

They were in Ellen's bedroom. The questions were repeated and repeated until Amanda could scarcely hold her patience. The mute girl merely stared, made no effort to reply, ignored the pad and pen on her bedside table.

But there was a look of urgency in her eyes.

She wants to tell me something, Amanda realized. Then why doesn't she write it down and give it to me to read?

When she asked that question, Ellen shook her head. With a deep sigh, Amanda began to ask again what she had asked so many times before.

"Does this piece of paper with the name Charlene on it mean anything to you? Did you write it?"

This time there was no quick shake of the head. Ellen hesitated for a long time and then slowly nodded. Amanda felt a little thrill of triumph. "Then you can tell me what it means!"

There was no movement from the girl in the bed this time. Only her eyes revealed anything. There was not only the serious look in them, but a look of pleading. She seemed to be begging Amanda not to go on with the questioning. But Amanda knew she must.

"The music? You know what that was all about?"

No answer and no change of expression.

"Did you smell Madame's perfume and guess that a bottle of it had been broken?"

There was a cautious nod. There was a stiffening of the slender body when Amanda asked, "Did you ever see a phantom — a ghost — around here in the middle of the night?" There was a vigorous shake of Ellen's head.

Both girls had awakened early. Both were tired from not having had enough sleep, and in Amanda's case at least, what little there had been was fitful and interrupted.

Now there was a long day to get through. At

95

nine o'clock, when she had finished showering and dressing and was on the way to Ellen's room, she heard Rick at the telephone. He was checking the time they would all gather in the music room for the reading of the will. He had known that it was to be at four o'clock, but, Amanda guessed, he was making sure that he did not remain at Chanson for one hour more than was necessary. Having confirmed the time of the will reading with Mr. Platt, his next call would undoubtedly be to the bus station to check the schedule. The thought depressed her. She and Rick had been close these past few days. To be sure, it had not been all pleasant, but they had shared something and she wondered if, after they left this place, they would ever see each other again.

Four o'clock seemed a long way off. That hour did not surprise her in any way. That had been Madame's social hour of the day. No matter where anyone was or what they happened to be doing at the time, everything had to be dropped. Everyone had to join Madame for tea in whatever room she had chosen that day.

Usually it was one of the smaller rooms: the back parlor, the study, or the music room where, on special occasions, she would sit at the baby grand piano and play a Chopin waltz or lively little songs of her native land.

Every day there would be what she called "high tea" with the second-best silver tea things gleaming in the late-afternoon sunshine, which came in through the long windows. There would be paper-thin sandwiches and scones and, for special treats, the delicious French pastry as only Matilde could make it.

It was a strange combination of English and French, and Amanda wondered about that now. A woman who clung tenaciously to the mores of her homeland, as Madame Bonheur did, might not be expected to follow those of another country. Nor, for that matter, to have an unexplainable fondness for Irish music, among the other kinds that seemed to have no rhyme or reason, either.

True, Madame had sometimes had guests during those weekends eight, nine, and ten years ago. Occasionally the piano could be heard in the early hours of the evenings, but Amanda could not remember anything that sounded like popular music being played.

She would make one more attempt with Ellen, she decided. Perhaps if Ellen knew that the inquisition was over she would consent to answer one question. She smiled coaxingly at Ellen and reached over and took her hand.

"That piece of paper. You left that there, didn't you? Sort of like how we used to play the treasure hunt game? I'm supposed to follow that clue?"

She thought she saw a faint movement of the girl's lips, something that had not happened in her presence since they had returned to Chanson. She wanted to believe that Ellen was trying to talk, but she had no knowledge of this sort of problem. She knew that she was on very delicate ground. She realized that at this moment she must not do or say the wrong thing.

She said to Ellen, "Don't get up yet if you don't

feel like it. I'm going to find Rick and we'll come right back. Today we're going to stick together."

But it was not as quick and easy as she had thought it was going to be.

She went downstairs and found the kitchen empty. When she had been there earlier, she had heard him in the study, telephoning to Roger Platt. He was not there now, nor in any of the downstairs rooms, which she looked into hastily.

In the kitchen, dark brown liquid bubbled in the coffee maker, a toaster stood on one of the counters with a loaf of bread beside it, a pitcher of orange juice was on the butcher-block table. But there was no dirty plate or cup and saucer or empty glass or silverware in sight.

Matilde could have washed them and put them away, which was to be expected for she always kept the kitchen neat, but why had she left the other things about?

Her firm, even footsteps sounded in the hall outside and then, after she came over the threshold, she stopped short. She was dressed for the day — black uniform, starched apron, flat-heeled, comfortable shoes.

Amanda, meeting that stern, angry look, felt as guilty as though she had been caught doing something wrong. Her face burned with a scalding flush.

"I was just looking for Rick," she stammered. "I know he's up. I heard him on the phone earlier. Has he already had his breakfast?"

"Some time ago. And he ate it in the dining room where Madame wishes her guests to be served." Matilde's lips were a straight line. "Even though she may not be here, the amenities must still be observed. And they will be as long as I am here to take care of this house."

Gazing into that strong, harsh face, Amanda's feeling of intimidation grew. She thought, Why, she sounds a little mad! It would not be surprising if Matilde had grown eccentric having lived in this remote, gloomy place alone for the past thirteen months.

She wondered what would happen to Matilde after the will was read and the estate disposed of. Certainly Madame Bonheur would have left her faithful housekeeper and companion a legacy that would provide for her for the rest of her life. Perhaps Chanson du Lac would belong to Matilde by this time tomorrow.

It might be all that Madame had left to give.

Amanda could not tell why that thought had popped into her head. She had never known the source of Madame's income. It could be that there were debts, which had accrued through the years, and what a good joke it would be on all of them if there were only small, token bequests to the young people — so small that they would provide only enough to cover the cost of their transportation to and from Lake Falls! She could not bear to think of that.

When Rick had disappeared for a long time on the other occasion, she had been unable to find him; he had claimed that he went for a walk. But this was no sort of day for a casual stroll. The fog had turned to drizzle. When Amanda went out onto the porch, she could barely see the lake at the bottom of the lawn. The boathouse was just a murky blur in the drizzle.

Somehow the weather seemed to match the day. Madame's death must come to all their minds. There was something sad about the fact that her house and belongings remained completely intact while their owner had been gone for more than a year. It was sobering, too — the prospect of learning whether a capricious old lady, whom none of them had really known, had cared for any of them except Carla, or had played a sly trick on them.

Amanda wished that Rick would put in an appearance. In spite of the fact that it was daytime, she felt something dark and menacing in the atmosphere. The last thing in the world she wanted to do was to go wandering about the house searching for Rick, as the two of them had done when they had been hunting for Ellen.

The rain looked as though it might continue for a long time. It was no sort of day, certainly, to be sloughing about outdoors. But Amanda had a feeling that he was out there somewhere and not very far away. He had the same sort of feeling she had about Chanson. He would not have lingered in it with nothing to do except wait for four o'clock to come.

She thought that to occupy her time, she would take a walk to the village, ignore the weather. When did a little rain ever hurt anyone? She went upstairs to get her raincoat and scarf. Then she went along the hall to Ellen's bedroom, undecided as to whether or not she should leave her alone.

But nothing had happened to Ellen, and she was either deeply asleep or pretending to be. Her silken lashes lay like tiny fans against the creamy, smooth skin, and her hair was golden against the snowiness of her pillow.

Amanda drew the satin quilt farther up onto Ellen's shoulders. Then she eased her conscience by convincing herself that she would be gone for only a little while, not more than an hour at the most. She went out and closed the door softly behind her.

The door to Madame's bedroom was closed. Without enough courage to open it, Amanda stood close to it and sniffed. She could smell no odor of violets now, but of course Matilde by this time would have cleaned up the mess made by the spilled perfume. How indignant she must have been at finding the shrinelike place desecrated! Yet she had not said a word about it when she and Amanda had met in the kitchen a short time ago.

Amanda would not let her mind linger on this new puzzle. She was not about to let herself worry about anything except keeping out of trouble until four o'clock.

A few minutes later she went downstairs and out onto the porch again. She walked down the steps and into the persistent drizzle. After a moment's hesitation, she turned away from the path that led down to the lake and started along the one that curved out to the road behind the house. The mist was so thick that she could see only a few feet ahead of her.

She had gone only a little way when she heard the sound of a car with its motor idling.

She stopped short. She knew that whoever owned the automobile she was hearing could not be Rick. He did not own one and would have had no reason to rent one for the few hours that still remained of their stay here.

A delivery van? But Amanda had learned that Matilde Gerard did her own shopping and carried home her own bundles. A guest? At this hour of the morning? And it was too early for Roger Platt.

Amanda stepped backward so that whoever was in the car would not see her, and she felt her feet sink into the spongy ground. The rain was wet upon her face, and she was conscious, for a minute or two, only of her discomfort.

Then the man who had left the car with its motor running came around the corner of the house and got into the driver's seat. Amanda recognized him. This was the same man who had been standing outside Chanson du Lac, looking up at its windows.

13.

SHE stood staring at the car, its red lights like cloudy rubies as it drove down the driveway and disappeared. She was so engrossed in wondering who the man was, what he was doing there, and why he had come so openly to Chanson in broad daylight that she did not hear someone come up behind her.

A voice at her ear spoke her name and caused her to jump, her heart bumping against her ribs.

When she turned and saw Michael Blake standing there, she could not have said whether she was more disappointed or relieved or angry.

"You!" she said coldly. "What are you doing here?"

"Running down a story," he told her. "What else? You didn't think I was going to give up all that easily, did you?"

She tried to tell him that there was no story, that he was wasting his time and might as well go home, but his voice drowned out hers.

"I'll settle for why you're out on a rotten day like this, and why you're standing here gawking after Pete Gregory while he's taking off. I'll settle for that for starters."

"Pete Gregory?" Her voice took on a note of excitement. "You mean you know him?"

"Sure, and have since I was a little kid. As a matter of fact, his wife and my mother . . ."

"Never mind that!" Amanda said impatiently. "Just tell me who he is and why he's hanging around here. This is the second time — "

Michael held up his hand. "Whoa, not so fast! I'm the one who asks the questions, remember? Something's going on here and I intend to find out what it is. I'm not going back to the office without the story — the whole story, and nothing but the story."

He raised his hand as though taking a solemn oath. There was a faint smile on his lips but his eyes were hard — and waiting.

"Tell ya what I'm gonna do," he said in a not-very-successful imitation of a sidewalk spieler. "We'll make a trade. You give me something I can use, and I'll give you the lowdown on Pete Gregory. Deal?"

She thought for a moment or two. Under no circumstances would she reveal to him anything about the late-night visits of the "phantom"; nor about the weird music that both she and Rick had heard; nor anything concerning having been pushed partially down the staircase.

But she knew that she would have to tell him something.

"Can't everything wait until after the will is read?"

"I have a twelve o'clock deadline for hard news," he told her. "And there are dailies in a couple of nearby towns. I don't want what everybody else prints."

"All right," she sighed. "Does the name Charlene mean anything to you?"

He pushed his rainproof hat back on his head and rubbed his forehead. In his belted trench coat, standing there in the mist, he looked very attractive, the way reporters should look but seldom did, she thought. Her resolve stiffened. She did not intend to be taken in by his coaxing smile, which died when she spoke the name.

"Charlene?" he repeated. "Charlene who?" He thought for a moment. "Couple of weeks ago the police picked up a shoplifter in one of the stores in the mall by that name. Can't remember the rest of it. I could be wrong. She might have been Marlene something."

"You," said Amanda testily, "are a great big help. Thanks a whole lot."

"No, but what has Charlene to do with anything?" he demanded. "You're not going to get any information from me about Pete Gregory unless you give me something in return. Okay?"

She spent a few minutes in serious thought. She had to tell him something — and it had to be important enough to satisfy him — and yet not give away anything about what had been happening in Solange Bonheur's house.

The treasure hunt seemed harmless enough. So she told him about the game she and Ellen and Carla had played on that summer afternoon almost ten years ago. When she mentioned Carla's name, Michael immediately found something that interested him.

"But she won't be there, this Carla Bonheur, when the will is read today. She'll be the only one of the grandchildren who won't be here to get her share. And how about this other girl? I've heard that she's a deaf mute."

"Not true!"

She could not remember ever having been so angry. She was appalled, too, at how facts could be twisted by people who actually didn't know what they were talking about.

"She's not a deaf mute!" she said furiously. "She's had a little trouble with her speech, but she can communicate with us well enough and she knows everything that goes on around her. And she's smart and sensitive, not like some people who don't think before they make stupid remarks!"

He held up his hands, palms out, as though to shield his face from expected blows. "Hey!" he said, sounding pleased. "You know what? You've got real spirit." He let his hands drop. "Any chance of our going out together some night? That guy with the scowl — the one who must be one of the heirs — anything serious going on between you? You're a little young for me, but I won't quibble over a couple of years. So how about it?"

"I won't be here after tonight." She told him

where she lived and added slyly, "Too far off, right? There's nothing like a four-hour bus ride to make you lose your enthusiasm. The traffic's a mess if you're planning to drive."

"Then let's grab each shining moment while we can. Or gather us rosebuds or something." He was deep in thought for a moment or two and then shook his head. "I don't know. There must be something wrong there. It doesn't seem to come out right."

She could not help giggling. And she realized that it was a long time since she had laughed at something a young man said — or at anything else for that matter. The lifting of her spirits was brief. It came and went quickly on that dark, gloomy day.

She tried to remember what had been in those clues that Carla had written on scraps of paper and hidden in various parts of the house. All that she could remember was the one that had led to the dead snake, and she certainly was not going to reveal anything about that to Michael Blake.

"The thing is that even if I could remember the clues, I'd never be able to recall the sequence they were in. There was something about Monsieur Bonheur's study." She closed her eyes and tried to bring into her mind a picture of that small room and the oversized desk, which seemed to take up most of the space.

Seeing it in her imagination, words suddenly popped into Amanda's brain.

"Now that you're here, take a look; you'll find what you seek hidden in a book!"

She said the words aloud, and Michael nodded.

"That sounds simple enough. But which book would it be? And how many of them are there?"

"Let's go and see."

She led him to the study and for the first time she saw him speechless. He gazed first at one wall and then another, his eyes going slowly up and then down again as he looked at the shelves of books that stretched almost to the ceiling. Finally he shook his head.

"Talk about the proverbial needle in a haystack! Where do we start for gosh sake? There must be a few thousand of these things here. So she put a clue here somewhere. In a book according to the rhyme. But which book?"

"It was a special one," Amanda said slowly. "Because, as I remember, it didn't take Ellen and me long to find the next clue. And it wasn't a regular volume. Not like these here." And she waved a hand at the nearest bookshelves. "More like a journal, perhaps a diary. I remember that Madame was angry when she found out that we had been playing with something that evidently was sacred in her eyes. It was one of the few times I heard her scold Carla."

"What was in it?" Michael demanded.

Now he was all business. The sophistication was gone, the slightly mocking manner vanished.

"I don't know," Amanda confessed. "And I don't know whether what we found here came before or after something important to the game. I'm sorry, Michael. It just doesn't come to me."

He grumbled a little but his complaints were not directed at her. He looked provoked for a few minutes, and then he moved toward the desk.

"Let's see if there's anything in there. That's where a diary or journal would be, right?"

"It's probably locked," she warned him. "And if it isn't, there's not much chance anything Monsieur owned would still be around. He's been dead for a long, long time."

She had been trying to warn him against disappointment, but he wasn't paying any attention to her. He was pulling at the knobs of the drawers, which stretched along the front of the desk.

"Right on that score," he said, straightening up. "They're all locked. Well, let's see what we can do with a little help."

He took a pen knife out of his pocket, and she began to protest. "You'd better not get a single scratch anywhere. If you do, Matilde will have your head. And if she finds you fooling around where you don't belong, well — I'll be sorry for you, that's all."

"Stop worrying. I'm an old breaker-in from way back when. Now let's see how this will work."

They were not to find out. For, at that moment, there was the sound of footsteps, which grew louder as they approached, and when Amanda and Michael turned toward the door, they saw Matilde and Rick standing on the threshold.

14.

IT would have been hard for Amanda to decide which of the two was the most outraged. Not that she blamed either of them. She and Rick had been a team, working together for the same purpose. It was all too plain that now there was someone else searching for clues to solve the mystery of Chanson du Lac. And of all people, this young man for whom Rick had taken an instant dislike!

To Matilde Gerard had fallen the responsibility for keeping the house in order and guarding its furnishings. It was no wonder that she was enraged at finding Amanda and a stranger poking into things that did not belong to them, in places where they had no right to be.

What Rick was thinking was hidden behind a tight and angry face. He turned quickly on his heel and strode away. Amanda longed to run after him and explain to him why she had been here with Michael Blake.

Matilde said furiously, "What is it you think you are doing, eh? There at Monsieur's desk, what did you hope to find? Sneaking about — did I not warn you about that just a short time ago, Miss? And this man here, who is he?"

She waved an arm at Michael and then went on without waiting for an answer. Matilde went on scolding, her voice rising and falling.

"You thought to find something of value in Monsieur's desk? I will tell you that you would have been disappointed. Nothing remains in it and has not for many years. After Monsieur's death, Madame had me clean out from it everything it contained. Some of it was put away in the safe in her bedroom. Other things of no importance were destroyed. What do you think of that, eh?"

Michael was edging toward the door. "Sounds like a family quarrel. No place for an outsider."

Matilde ignored him. She went on speaking to Amanda. "I came to tell you that I have prepared luncheon, and it will be served in the breakfast room. I would advise you to eat. I shall not remain to cook dinner for all those who will be here late this afternoon. Once the will is read I shall be gone."

To where? Amanda wondered, but she did not ask the question aloud. This had been her home for the greater part of her life. Chanson, as part of the estate, might have to be sold. Surely Madame would have made some provisions for Matilde.

Michael, who had almost reached the door, inquired, "Am I wrong in jumping to the conclusion that I am not invited to stay for lunch? It just so happens that I am free."

Matilde threw him a contemptuous look but did not reply. When he seemed to be about to say more, Amanda shook her head at him. It was necessary for her to placate Matilde, and she did not know how to go about it.

"It was a game," she said coaxingly. "We didn't intend to hurt anything."

"A game," Matilde repeated. "I am growing sick of your games, Miss. Pretending about things which do not happen. Trying to say you have seen her — which, of course, was out-and-out lie. Music, is it, that plays in the night which never could be so!"

It was the first time Amanda had seen Matilde actually lose her temper. There had been times when she had raised her voice to them; scolding had been a routine thing. But never had her face turned this alarming shade of scarlet. And her eyes seemed to bulge; it was plain that she had lost every vestige of self-control. Otherwise she would not have cried out the things she did in front of a stranger.

When she paused for breath he muttered, "Very interesting!" A wad of copy paper and a ballpoint pen came out of his pocket. "Now," he asked Matilde courteously, "wouldn't you like to tell me all about everything? Let's start with the girl who disappeared eight years ago and hasn't been seen since. There was such a girl, wasn't there? And I've got the date right?"

Fear made Matilde's face crumble. It appeared, glittering, in her eyes. "Get out!" she choked. "If I see you around again, I shall call the police."

He looked from her to Amanda and then back again. Finally he shrugged his shoulders and turned. His footsteps sounded in the hall, and then he was gone. And Amanda did not remember until then that he had not kept his part of the bargain and told her who Pete Gregory was.

Neither Rick nor Ellen came to lunch in the breakfast room. Amanda was relieved. She felt that she couldn't have endured an hour of sitting opposite either of them, trying to keep up her end of meaningless conversation exactly as though this were an ordinary day. Rick would be sullen; Ellen would go on hiding what she knew — and Amanda was certain that she did know something — acting, for perhaps the first time in her life, deceitfully.

It was not a very good luncheon. It seemed to be made up of scraps and leftovers, the sort prepared by someone who is going away and wants to use up whatever is in the refrigerator.

Matilde was dressed for the gathering in the music room. She wore a black serge skirt of an unfashionable length, a starched blouse, and patent leather pumps. She had dabbed rouge on her cheeks and traced her lips with a matching shade of red. She did not look at all like her usual self, and Amanda thought, a little wryly, that perhaps this other Matilde was not so unbending and unfriendly.

It must be an important day for her, too; less than three hours remained until she would know whether her service to her mistress had been appreciated, or if all her dreams of security in her later years had been merely that — dreams.

"Matilde," Amanda asked impulsively, "what will you do? After today, I mean. Do you have a family somewhere? Or is there some place where you'd want to live? Or will you stay here?"

For a moment, the woman's face seemed to soften. It was not often, Amanda guessed, that anyone had expressed concern about her. She'd been devoted to Madame and to Carla. There had been no one else, as far as Amanda knew. She had never seen a guest in Matilde's kitchen. During the times Madame entertained, there had been additions to the staff, hired waiters and serving girls. But they had come and gone. None had stayed for more than a day or two.

Matilde did not answer Amanda's questions. She had seemed about to speak but evidently thought better of it. She swept up the dishes from the table and hurried into the kitchen with them. Amanda heard the sound of the dishwasher starting up, and there was something final about the sound, which lowered her spirits. In a little while now, less than three hours, everything of Chanson du Lac would be over for her. Good-byes would be said. She would be seeing the house for the last time.

When she went out into the kitchen, the dishwasher was still running, but Matilde was nowhere in sight. Packing, Amanda thought. Matilde must have accumulated a large number of possessions during her many years here. But where were Rick and Ellen? She was about to go upstairs and see if Ellen was in her room when she noticed that a door on the other side of the kitchen was slightly ajar. From somewhere beyond it, she heard someone calling her name.

She went cautiously to the door and opened it farther. She peered down into darkness. While she waited there at the top of the cellar steps, her heart began to beat hard and rapidly. And then she heard the voice again.

"Amanda! Amanda!"

She could not tell whether it was a man or a woman, a girl or a boy who was calling. There was a false sound about that voice, as though someone were bent on disguising it.

Amanda had not the slightest intention of going down into that pitch-black place where no light of any kind shone. She stood on the top step, waiting to see if whoever was down there would identify himself or herself. If there was nothing like that, she would find someone to accompany her downstairs. She did not care whom she managed to enlist for that purpose — Matilde, Rick, even Michael Blake.

There was a sudden flare of dazzling light, and it blinded her. It was as though all the brilliance in the world was shining in her eyes. She could see nothing and, as she threw out her hand to grasp at the wooden banister at her right, she lost her balance and stumbled down the remainder of the steps.

And the light went out.

For a moment or two all that Amanda could see were the dancing, brilliant pinpoints of light still shining behind her eyes. She put up a hand to cover them and staggered again, this time against the bottom step of the flight of wooden stairs. She caught herself before she fell, not being able to see anything now, not even leftover, tiny stars of brightness.

She was enveloped in complete darkness; it was as though she were wrapped in a black blanket that covered every bit of her body. Her vision slowly adjusted to the darkness, and she grasped the wooden handrail, and slowly putting one foot carefully above the other, pulled herself up the steps.

She could see the outline of the door, closed now — and for one horrible instant she thought, What if it's locked! Suppose someone tricked me into coming down here and then locked me in?

It was a dreadful thought. She was being silly and senseless. She knew what she must do — reach the door above her, open it, and find a flashlight if there was no electrical switch at the top of the stairs. That great, blinding light had come from somewhere. The person who had called her name must still be down there somewhere, although the voice was silent now.

Twice she stopped and listened. She was not going to be foolhardy and try to find anyone in that dark vacuum. The light switch. The flashlight. The return to the cellar with Matilde or preferably Rick, or, if she could persuade neither of them to go with her, Ellen as a last resort.

Amanda had it all planned. But she couldn't get out of the cellar soon enough. She drew a great sigh of thankfulness when she reached the door and grasped its handle.

The planning, the sensible attitude, the reassurance she had tried to give to herself — all of it was meaningless.

For the door to the kitchen was locked.

15.

*B*UT it could not be. She had been imagining the door being locked, and so she was still in the grip of that fantasy. This she told herself as she grasped the doorknob and tried to turn it again.

It resisted her efforts. It did not move an inch in either direction.

She tried to remember how the door had looked from the other side when she had found it partly open. Had there been a bolt on it, a bolt that someone had pushed into place after she had stepped out onto the first step of the staircase? Perhaps it had been done when she had been struggling to hold her balance. She had been too absorbed in trying to keep from plunging down the steps.

She began to call out. Her voice rose and fell as she called Matilde's name, for if anyone were in the kitchen, it would be Matilde. But the woman had been dressed for the street the last time

Amanda had seen her, through with her kitchen chores. It was doubtful that she would linger about there if her work was finished.

Amanda could feel panic rising inside her. It would have been all too easy to succumb to hysteria. She knew that someone was down there, the someone who had called to her and was in hiding somewhere waiting to . . .

Waiting to do what?

She threw herself on the door once more, pounding upon it until her hands began to ache. She cried out Matilde's name over and over until she was hoarse. She would scream at the top of her lungs, stop and listen for a moment or two, draw a deep breath, and then begin shrieking again.

During one of those brief respites she heard something from a far corner of the cellar. It was a loud, harsh sound and all she could compare it to was that of something falling. She called out, but whoever was over there in the darkness did not answer her.

She was beginning to think a little more lucidly now. There had to be a light somewhere, and if she was very careful, if she did not move into strange places and fall into a new trap, she could find it.

When her hand touched a light switch on the wall, she was so relieved she could have burst into tears. She flipped the button upward and nothing happened. The electricity had evidently been turned off.

There was no point in standing there flicking the switch on and off, or screaming out for help when no one was going to come from the kitchen door. She turned and looked down into that dark cavern. There was a window back there that was high up in the wall. It was a narrow octagon only a little brighter on this dark and drizzly day than the wall surrounding it.

She did not think that would be of any help. She would not be able to reach it even with the help of a chair, or a stepladder, or some other article of furniture she might be able to find. She was not about to risk falling.

Her mind cleared and she realized she was being ridiculous thinking about the danger of falling, although there was nothing to fall from. She should be trying to figure out a way of making someone upstairs realize her predicament, and praying that that person would not be the one who had locked her into this dark, dank place. The thought of rats and other small creatures who might have made their home in the cellar of Chanson du Lac made her feel sick with terror. She listened but heard nothing — no sound of scratching or faint squeaks.

Score one for our side, she thought wildly, knowing that she was becoming giddy and making a strong effort at self-control. There had to be more than one door in this large area. She must find it.

The basement of the house was far-flung, every ell having its own foundation so that it was almost like a maze that she would have to find her way out of. She had left the part of the cellar that was under the kitchen and was now standing below the dining room. There was a dumbwaiter in the butler's pantry. Someone in that vicinity would surely hear her if she screamed loudly enough.

But no one did.

When she turned a corner she came upon another window, the one too high to reach, also. A moment later, she tripped over something and her heart rose swiftly with hope.

Steps! She had found the outside cellar door.

She could tell what it was by running her hand along the sloping, wooden surface. During one of those summers when she had come here as a child, Madame had had a part-time handyman and gardener. Mr. Scolamino — the name came back to her easily. Funny, she mused, that you could remember the most trivial things and forget the really important ones. At any rate, on several occasions Amanda had seen Mr. Scolamino working on the lawn and pruning the shrubbery. He had been in and out of the cellar, which was where the gardening tools were kept, and he had left the cellar door open.

Thank you, Mr. Scolamino, Amanda said silently. Then, not much later, she discovered that she had nothing to thank the man for. She could not find the way to open the cellar doors.

She tried as she had never tried anything before in her life, pulling until her hands, already sore from so much pounding, became useless. She could have sunk down on the steps right then and there and wept with disappointment and frustration.

Something gave her strength to move on, careful to avoid anything in her path. There were all sorts of things cluttering that part of the cellar:

discarded furniture, cartons with old clothing spilling out from them, an aged sewing machine. By the dusty light from the window above her head, Amanda could dimly see those things.

When she turned another corner, she found she had reached a dead end. There was nowhere to go from there. What was beyond the wall was evidently the grounds of Chanson du Lac, but she had run out of hope. She had come to the end of that, too.

There had been a dense stillness surrounding her since she had come into the cellar. Even her own breathing had been quiet. Now she was aware that the silence had been broken. She gasped and the sound was overly loud, seeming to have been magnified a hundred times over.

What she heard was the flowing of water. There was no mistaking it. And it was not the light dripping of a faucet; it was the noise of a small-scale flood somewhere above her head, where pipes ran along the high ceiling and into the old-fashioned furnace.

Somewhere there must be a water pipe, she knew. But what could she do if she found it? How could she stop the flow of perhaps boiling-hot water?

But there would be no scalding liquid. Both she and Rick had discovered that the boiler worked only at certain hours of the day. Small consolation, she thought. Would it be more pleasant to die in comfort?

For die she would. There was no way of escaping from this prison she had been thrust into. The water would rise and rise and she would drown in this awful, cold, damp place and it might be days before she was found.

Days? Who would find her? They would all be gone by evening — Rick and Ellen and, without doubt, Matilde Gerard. They might wonder at her disappearance, especially when there was money involved, but did they care enough to institute a thorough search?

Tears of self-pity forced their way out of her eyes. She rubbed them away, not caring that her hands were dirty and that she was making a mess of her face. What difference did that make now?

She wondered about the time. Even if it had been light enough to see a dial, she had no watch with her; she had left it upstairs on the dresser in her bedroom. She had no way of telling how long she had been in this damp and dreadful place. It seemed like hours. The time for Madame's heirs to be gathering in the music room must certainly be at hand.

Wouldn't they miss her? Wouldn't someone turn and inquire, "Where's Amanda?"

She huddled close to the door at the top of the stairs. Expecting nothing to come of it, but so desperate she had to give it a try, she opened her mouth and screamed as loudly as she possibly could.

As though that had been a signal of some sort, the lights in the cellar went on.

16.

SOMEONE had turned on the switch in the kitchen or the utility room — the same person, no doubt, who had turned them off.

She grasped the doorknob, intending to rattle it to capture the attention of whoever was on the other side of the door. It moved easily in her hand, and she was able to turn it far to the right. As she did, the door creaked open.

When she walked into the kitchen, her eyes had not adjusted to the contrast between darkness and light. She blinked and groped her way to the nearest chair and clung to its back. When her vision cleared, she saw that the kitchen was empty.

She had no idea how the electrical system in a big house like Chanson du Lac worked, at what point it could be manipulated to turn on lights and appliances all over the house. She tiptoed across the kitchen as though she expected that the wrong move might plunge the house into darkness.

But where was everyone? There was a death-like hush over everything. Still walking quietly, she went through the butler's pantry and down the hall to the front entrance. Beside the door there was a suitcase she guessed must belong to Matilde. Rick and Ellen, like herself, had brought their belongings in tote bags. This piece of luggage was the old-fashioned kind, of bulging leather and held by strong straps. Matilde, it seemed, was not going to lose any time. Once the will was read, she would be leaving immediately. She would not be making one more trip upstairs.

The grandfather clock on the first landing of the staircase boomed three times. So Amanda knew that she had been down in the cellar for not quite an hour. And there was still one more hour before she would be able to leave Chanson. The time could not pass quickly enough.

Where were the others? What had Ellen and Rick been doing while she had been locked in that dreadful place that they had not heard her calling and pounding on the door?

She walked the few steps to the music room, looking up into it for the last time before they would all gather in it to hear what an imperious old lady had done to their lives. Amanda had never speculated upon Madame's wealth. She had simply taken it for granted that there would be money. It was beginning to seem as though, after what she had been through, it was earned the hard way.

The music room was neat now. Sheet music was piled in stacks as there had been before, but when Amanda went to inspect them, she saw that they had been rearranged. Those on top of the piles were different from what she had seen before.

The picture of the Irish colleen was nowhere in sight. Taking its place was the picture of a very pretty Indian girl. The title of the song was "My Little Redwing."

Throughout the room substitutions had been made, instruments had been put away, the table that had been in front of the window had been pushed aside, and the old-fashioned autoharp was nowhere in sight.

A row of chairs formed a semicircle, which faced a low platform. There, without doubt, Roger Platt would stand when he read what Madame had ordered written. Amanda had seen Mr. Platt only a few times, when he had come to Chanson while she had been staying there. She knew nothing about him except that he was young; she remembered Matilda having said that in a grumbling sort of voice.

For a little while he would be important in their lives and then she would never see him again. He would fade out of her memory just as would Matilde and Chanson and the briefly known Michael Blake. And Ellen and Rick? Was her friendship with them to come to an end by the time the day was over?

She was so preoccupied with the thought of parting with the Stantons that she did not hear the sound of footsteps along the hall. When someone spoke to her, she started — then bit back a cry as she whirled.

Matilde, still dressed in her street clothes and therefore looking unfamiliar, said reprovingly, "There will be nothing to do here for one hour, Miss."

"Do you object to my being here until then? Is there any reason why I should not remain in this room?"

She had not meant her voice to sound insolent. She had never answered Matilde back when she had scolded. But Amanda's nerves were frazzled. She was still shaky from her session in the cellar and completely ready to believe that Madame's housekeeper had been the one who had subjected her to the awful ordeal.

She stared directly into Matilde's face. "It was you, wasn't it? You were the one!"

Whatever the woman was thinking and feeling was immediately hidden. Her face became mask-like. Her eyes grew expressionless.

"I do not know what you are talking about."

"I am talking," Amanda said stonily, "about being locked in the cellar after someone pushed me into it. Someone who turned off the electricity so that everything was dark, who somehow made it sound as though the place would be flooded. When that someone decided it was time for me to leave, I was let out. Nothing had really happened to me except that I was scared half to death."

She had become out of breath, but there was nothing more she could say to Matilde. If only the woman would admit to this latest trick, it should not be too hard to get a confession from her that she had been at the bottom of all the other terrifying happenings.

But Matilde wasn't going to admit to anything. There was still that fixed stare, the mouth so tight that it appeared as though it would never utter another word.

"Tell me," Amanda coaxed, "why whatever it is that's been going on around here has all been aimed at me. We have maybe fifty minutes left. If I knew the reason for all this crazy business — "

And then Matilde did speak. The glaze left her eyes, and they became a little wild. "I don't believe any of it, not any at all! You've been telling lies since the minute you walked in here. Do you want to know what I think? Well, I will tell you. I believe that you are freaked out."

Amanda felt her jaw fall open. She leaned forward a little as though to prove to herself that she had actually heard what Matilde had said.

"Freaked out." Where in the world had Matilde picked up that bit of slang?

It seemed that this was Matilde's breaking point. Everything that had been bottled up inside her suddenly began to pour out, and what she said was almost incoherent, a mixture of English, some type of Provençal French, and idioms Amanda could not translate.

Matilde seemed on the brink of hysteria, and Amanda grasped the woman's shoulders and shook her roughly.

"Calm down," she said in a voice that could scarcely be heard over Matilde's. "If there is something you wish to tell me — "

"No, no! There is nothing!"

"We are not going back to that. You have told me too much to stop now, but not enough so I can make any sense of it. Matilde, who is doing these terrible things to me? I know that you know. There's not much time left until four o'clock, and I'm not afraid that something will happen to me before then. I'm not even sure anything actually was meant to happen to me. What was it all about?"

The woman began to babble. "It was for her — always for her! Now where is she?"

"Dead," Amanda ventured. "You are speaking of Madame, of course?" But Matilde went on rapidly, as though there was not enough time to say what she wished to say.

"It is the man! I never liked him. And there was the house, and I wanted to follow Madame's wishes in that. This seemed the best, the only way there was."

She drew a sobbing breath. "Spoiled! All of it spoiled because of him. Everything came out wrong! How Madame would have hated that! But I tried my best, as little as I liked it."

"What was it," Amanda asked, "that Madame would have wanted? Tell me, Matilde. Start with that."

"The condominiums. How she despised them! It was the ruination of our calm little village. Poor Madame!" And she shook her head sadly. "The house! She was so afraid that somehow it would fall into the wrong hands and be torn down to make room for a group of them here on the lake-front. She believed she had arranged things so that it could never happen." She began to weep quietly in a way that sounded as though her heart was breaking. "All her plans went awry."

"Matilde . . ." Amanda spoke very gently to the weeping woman. "She is dead, isn't she? And buried in Elm Grove Cemetery and has been there for more than a year?"

Her head coming up quickly, she cried, "But of course that is so! How could you not think so?" A look of understanding changed her face. "You are thinking now of the visits of a strange woman to your bedroom at night, eh? It was not Madame, of course."

"It was you!"

"*Non!*"

The accusation seemed to agitate Matilde to a greater degree than anything so far. Her reaction was frightening. Having said that one word, she did not seem able to speak another. Her mouth, the lips a terrifying shade of blue, opened and shut, but no word came through them. Her eyes fell back in her head.

Amanda moved quickly over the space that separated them. She knew that Matilde must draw air into her lungs, but there was little in the music room. The windows were large and heavy. She did not believe she would be able to get them open and hold Matilde at the same time. The front door seemed a quicker, easier way to get the woman to a place where she could breathe.

Matilde uttered a single word as Amanda propelled her to the door. She said "Madame" over and over again. Her feet were unsteady, and Amanda felt a sharp pang of pity. This woman who had been so brisk, so much in command of herself, grew sick and helpless before her eyes.

They were outside at last, and Amanda lowered Matilde down on a wicker chair that had not been put away at the summer's end. For some reason, that made her think of the dock and the boats tethered to it. She looked in that direction, and what she saw froze her in immobility.

17.

*I*T was like watching something in a horror show through a heavy veil. Because of the mist the two figures on the dock had a look of unreality, a ghostly look.

Not a sound could be heard, not because everything was being muffled by the thin rain, but because one of the figures was Ellen. Although her mouth was open as though she were screaming, nothing at all could be heard.

The other figure, taller by at least a head, wore a raincoat belted tightly, and it was difficult to tell at first if its wearer was a man or a woman. Then, as she tried to pull Ellen toward the end of the dock, her rain hat fell off, and Amanda had a glimpse of her face and knew in that moment who had instituted the campaign of terror against her.

Matilde had got to her feet and stood clinging to the porch railing. She cried out in protest but the drama on the dock went on, the struggle between the two growing more fierce.

Amanda began to run in their direction, kicking off her shoes as she went. She scarcely felt the wet grass under her feet. Everything seemed unreal, like something in a dream that kept repeating itself. It had been a day like this one, eight years ago, when Carla had pushed Ellen off the dock, but then the younger girl had been unaware that someone was behind her — she had gone into the lake in what was supposed to have been an accident.

This time she was fighting. She managed to get an arm free, and she tried to strike out at her assailant, but the woman was bigger and stronger. She put her hands under Ellen's arms and began to drag her farther and farther toward the edge of the dock. Neither noticed Amanda, who was racing in their direction, nor heard her when she called out.

It was like some sort of horrible drama in pantomime. It was like a dream in which she tried to make herself heard but couldn't, and tried to run fast but seemed not to be moving at all.

They were at the edge of the short pier now. Amanda saw Ellen lifted to her feet and for a moment it seemed like both she and the woman grasping her would go into the water. But only one went over the side. There was a great splash as Ellen went into the lake.

From somewhere Matilde's voice rose in a scream. Then there were other voices, but Amanda did not try to sort them out. She was waiting for

Ellen to come to the surface so that when she jumped in, she would land in an empty space. She took off her raincoat.

When she saw the drenched, flattened hair come into view, she took a few steps forward and dove cleanly into a spot beyond the girl who was thrashing about and gasping — filling her lungs with water.

Amanda's skirt hampered her. It rose as she came to the surface and ballooned around her. Her hair fell over her eyes and she pushed it back from her face, treading water as she looked about for Ellen.

She was only a few feet away, but she was thrashing about in a panic-stricken way and adding to the danger of drowning. Her hands grasped at nothing, and she sank once more.

Amanda knew that she must save her — poor little Ellen who hated and feared the water so much that she had never learned how to swim!

With her strong, even stroke Amanda reached her. Ellen's hands went out, grabbed at Amanda's shoulders and then her neck. Her grasp was so tight that Amanda could not draw a breath. Along with trying to keep them both afloat, there was the danger of choking to death, for Ellen was, in her terror, pressing harder and harder against Amanda's windpipe.

She had to strike her. There was no other way. She curled her fingers into a fist and took aim at Ellen's chin. It was not a hard blow, but it caused Ellen to loosen her hold. She did not fight when Amanda grasped her about the collar of her blouse and swam with her to the shallow part of the lakefront. There she put the unconscious girl down on the sand and collapsed beside her.

Somewhere, over to the right and above her, there was noise. Voices rose and fell, she heard running footsteps on the wooden dock. There were others, spongy ones; then someone said, "One's okay. But we better see if we can get the water out of this one. I'll be doing it while you get over to my car and call on the C.B. Here, take my keys."

It was a strange voice. There were more footsteps and when she sat up, Amanda could see Ellen's flattened body and a man who looked vaguely familiar giving her artificial resuscitation.

She tried to get to her feet but she fell back weakly. Her mind was in a turmoil. When she saw Ellen stir, she could have wept with joy. The man whom she didn't know went on with the steady, even pressing of his hands against the girl's ribs.

And then there were others around him. Michael Blake had gone to his car to call his paper with the first bulletin about the accident. Now he was back. Matilde was there looking stricken. But there was no sign of Rick. Amanda kept craning her neck, looking in the direction of the dock, but he seemed to be nowhere about. *Nor was Carla.*

Michael began to write furiously again, his face a study in concentration. Amanda spoke to him but he did not answer. She raised her voice, and the man who was forcing Ellen to sit up was the one who answered her.

"You won't get anything out of him, Miss. I'm Pete Gregory and I'm in real estate. I've been here looking over the property now and then, and I guess you wondered about that. I wanted to be on hand in case the house went up for sale after the will was probated. Lucky I happened along. I meant to speak to you, or someone, later. I had the inside track with Roger Platt, but now I understand he's not one of the heirs. Rotten luck!"

Amanda stared at him in disbelief. A girl had almost died. Someone had tried to kill Ellen. And yet here he was, speaking calmly in a voice so matter of fact, as though nothing unusual had happened, and it was business as usual with him.

Michael Blake stopped writing only long enough to ask Mr. Gregory if he knew how old the house was and didn't it have a name of some sort?

Amanda looked around in desperation. Somewhere, not very far away by now, Carla Bonheur was running from her attempt to drown a small, helpless girl.

And where was Rick?

Where had he been while all this was going on?

Michael Blake paused in his writing, went to his car, and came back with a blanket. Amanda refused it with a shake of her head, so he gave it to Mr. Gregory, who wrapped it around Ellen. It was as though this were just a simple, unfortunate accident. It would be reported to the police, if Michael had not already done so, as were all accidents. Amanda remembered all too well how it had been when the lake had been dragged for Carla's body. And all the time she had been alive and evidently in hiding.

Amanda squatted down beside Ellen. The girl gazed up into her face with expressionless eyes, which hid whatever she was thinking and feeling. Amanda picked up a limp hand and rubbed it gently. She was suddenly angry, and she straightened up and said to Mr. Gregory, "Ellen was pushed, you know. Carla threw her into the lake. Didn't you see that?"

All he had seen, he said, was the struggle of one girl to save another as they thrashed about in the water. He had come upon the scene to see how they happened to be in it.

"She pushed her," Amanda said doggedly. "Just as she did eight years ago. That time it was just a mean, nasty trick. This time, I think, she meant her to drown."

Matilde had been wringing her hands and babbling words and sentences that made no sense. Now she moved to the little group gathered around Ellen.

"It was an accident!"

They all turned toward her, Michael's pen halted, and Mr. Gregory took a pipe out of his pocket and put it in his mouth but did not light it.

"She stumbled on the dock. Carla was nowhere near her." Matilde pointed an accusing finger at Amanda. "She is only trying to start trouble."

Amanda cried, "That is not true!"

Matilde's voice had grown even. To see her standing there in the light drizzle, no longer looking like a ghostly figure, but somehow the stolid, devoted servant, it was almost impossible to believe that she was telling a monstrous lie.

"She is mad, that one," Matilde said. "You may find out for yourself if you speak more to her. Her mind is sick, and she may tell you about some wild fancies she has had — about the return from the dead of a woman who was buried a year ago, of hearing music not played by human hands, of someone trying to take her life. Can you tell me that those are not the ravings of a demented person?"

Amanda heard it with rising horror. Her face flushed, she knew that the hot rush of color was making her look guilty. Their silent stares were worse than if they had accused her outright.

She began to shiver. It was not only the wet clinging clothes and the light rain that chilled her. The drizzle had thinned out since she had left the house, and now she could see the dock fairly clearly; and in desperation her eyes kept going in its direction. She refused to believe that Rick was not somewhere near and hoped he would appear at any minute to confirm her story of what had actually happened.

Something was different about that short, wooden pier that stretched out into the water, but nothing transferred itself from her eyes to her mind. Perhaps it looked different because she was seeing it in the rain. There was no time to puzzle it out. Matilde was going on and on telling Mr. Gregory about the girl's "queerness," the fantastic tales she had told about her life having been in danger, her imprisonment in the cellar, and having nearly plunged down the main staircase.

Had she told Matilde about that last near-accident? It did not matter now. The things

Amanda had revealed to her were enough to back up Matilde's claims. She could not deny them, she realized with a sinking heart.

She had no one to stand with her and say that she was telling the truth. The two men hearing it all were concerned with their own affairs, even now. Mr. Gregory would evidently accept anything anyone might tell him, if that person happened to be in a position to help him get his hands on a valuable piece of property.

Michael Blake would accept Matilde's version of what had happened at Chanson du Lac, because the story of a mad heiress in the old house would make a first-class article.

"So," Matilde was saying, "I will recommend to those who ask me that this poor creature be put away where she can harm neither herself nor anyone else."

"Oh, no!" Amanda cried out without realizing she was doing so. She did not know where to turn or where to run to. It did not matter. Wherever she went, she must face her accusers.

Ellen stood up suddenly and pulled the blanket about her. Her mouth moved as it sometimes did when she wanted to say something and was frustrated because she could not.

This time she could. Her voice was loud and clear as she said, "She pushed me!"

18.

AFTER the first moment of stunned silence, Matilde cried out that it was a miracle. She kept repeating the word and then her voice lowered and she murmured about *"le bon Dieu."* She seemed about to sink to her knees, but she tottered over to where Ellen was standing and touched her, as though she could not believe what she had heard.

Amanda was speechless as she stared at the girl who had spoken after eight long years of not being able to do so. She did not stop to try to figure out what had happened. Ellen had spoken. That was all that mattered.

Ellen stood in her dripping clothing, and she was smiling as though extremely proud of herself. Amanda did not dare to press her to speak again, afraid that this might have been some sort of bizarre outburst, which would not be heard again.

The two men looked from one girl to the other. It was plain that Michael Blake had a dozen questions, but he saw the expression on Amanda's face and did not ask them. Mr. Gregory wore a puzzled frown.

"You take my advice you get this little girl in dry clothes," he said. "She doesn't need a bout of pneumonia. Best you should put her in bed for a while. Give her something hot to drink."

But there was not time for all that. Amanda wanted to tell him so, but he was busy wrapping the blanket more firmly around Ellen.

Amanda could not stop shivering, and when she tried to speak, her teeth chattered so that she could not be understood. It was almost as though her role and Ellen's had been reversed. Now she was the silent one, but she had to force the words out while the little group started up the path leading to the house.

"Ellen!" — Amanda's voice trembled with urgency — "where is Rick?"

The girl stopped short. Then, forming her lips carefully like a small child learning to talk, she said, "I do not know."

"But I haven't seen him for hours. Ellen, please! I am worried about him. It will soon be four o'clock, but it's not only that. He wouldn't stay away that long when he knew that I was . . . I was . . ."

She had been about to say "in danger," but there was Michael Blake tagging along with his pen and copy paper, and Mr. Gregory helping Ellen walk with the blanket around her and not missing anything that was being said.

"I wouldn't," he advised Amanda. "You don't want to upset her more."

"But there are important things!" Amanda was growing desperate. "Somebody may . . . " She put herself in front of Ellen and began to walk backward, so that she was in the line of the girl's vision. "Where were you when we were looking for you?"

"It's a big house," Ellen said in that careful, deliberate manner. "And there were things I had to know, had to find out. I wanted to make sure. Oh, yes, Amanda, I knew you were searching for me. As for Rick, I didn't see him after he went off with Carla."

Amanda felt as though an icy wind had swept down upon her and frozen every inch of her body.

"Carla!"

She said the name in a hoarse whisper and heard it repeated by Matilde. Immediately the woman began to bridle.

She ran along beside the others, babbling. Amanda tried not to listen, but she could not close her ears. Matilde was insisting that Carla was innocent of all wrongdoing. It was finally Ellen who interrupted her.

"She has run away — for now. But I am sure she will be back for the reading of the will. And if you are right, Matilde . . . " She did not finish the sentence. A strong fit of shivering overtook her. She had difficulty, even with Mr. Gregory's help, in getting up the staircase.

The grandfather clock on the stairway landing was booming four o'clock when Amanda and

Ellen went into the music room. They'd had had showers, and they were wearing clean blouses and slacks. Shampoos and brushing had brought a bright sheen to their hair.

Matilde was already there, sitting in a corner. She did not look up when the two girls entered. Her face was sober and troubled, as though she were undecided about some important problem.

Michael Blake and Mr. Gregory were waiting in the study down the hall. Michael was eager for the ending of his news story. The older man seemed intent on missing nothing that was to take place from then on.

Finally Roger Platt arrived. The front door was unlocked, and he came striding into the room with the assured manner of a person who knew where he was and why he was there.

He was a tall man with tight curly hair and a long face, which missed attractiveness by the slimmest of margins. His features were too close together and his chin was too long.

He greeted the others with a brief "So here we are!" and then put his briefcase on the table in front of him. Next he unlocked it and took out some papers.

He spoke then at more length. He told his listeners that they were to hear the last will and testament of Madame Solange Bonheur. He gave the date upon which it had been drawn up and explained certain provisions in the bequests.

He swept a brief glance around the room. Amanda, who had seen him only a few times when she had been younger, wondered why she had not noticed before that, although he appeared quite good-looking at first glance, he actually had a disagreeable expression.

His voice was flat and had a twang to it. He was explaining under what circumstances the legatees mentioned in the will would be unable to inherit.

"Confinement in a prison or mental facility. Failure to appear at the reading of the will. If certain heirs are eliminated, the money bequeathed to him or her will be divided among the others."

Amanda slid her hand into Ellen's and squeezed it. She could feel the tenseness of the girl beside her and wished that she could console her. It was doubtful now that Rick would show up in time to hear Roger Platt's formal reading of the will, but if he did not, both her's and Ellen's share would be larger. She did not want that. She wanted an end to all the tension and suspense, the worry about Rick, the atmosphere of something evil that had crept into the music room.

Even the self-possessed Mr. Platt appeared hurried and eager to be finished with the business at hand. He shuffled his papers around, found what he was looking for, and said, "Ah, yes, here we are."

At that moment there was a commotion in the hall outside. Voices, one shrill, and one deep and harsh, had the sound of quarreling. Mr. Platt stopped speaking. His eyes and those of the others turned toward the door. Two people came through it. Rick had his hand around the girl's wrist and was pulling her — not at all gently — after him.

And that was how Amanda saw Carla after eight years, her hair streaming around her face, her face distorted as she tried to wrench out of Rick's grasp. She was making strange sounds in her throat, almost like those of a trapped animal. She threw back her head suddenly, and she glared at Roger Platt whose jaw had fallen open. The sheaf of papers fell from his nerveless hands and he blurted, "What happened?"

She finally pulled herself free and she shrieked at him, "You blew it, that's what happened. You and your clever schemes! You said it would be easy! One pushed into the crazy house and another kept from showing up in time. And the other one" — she fastened her malevolent gaze on Ellen — "the little snoop, she found out too much. She should have stayed in the water!"

Amanda put her hands over her eyes as though she could close out the horrible realization that was flooding over her. Now she knew where Carla had been for the past eight years, back and forth to Chanson du Lac when she wanted something from Matilde who would have done anything Carla asked her to do. Perhaps to also see Roger Platt, who was doubtlessly in love with her, hoping that she would marry him and settle down.

Amanda's glance went from one to the other, and she saw that Carla had not lost faith in her ability to charm her way out of any situation.

"Rick," Carla said slanting a glance up at him. "You know it was only a trick. You didn't really think we were going to leave you out in the middle of the lake without oars, did you? Don't you remember when we were kids we were always playing jokes on each other?"

"Some joke!" He sounded enraged. He released

her hand and touched the back of his head with careful fingers. "What made you think you could get away with that?" Then he said to the room at large, "I suspected that she was around somewhere. That's what I was doing most of the morning, trying to track her down. Well, I found her all right, and wished I hadn't," he added ruefully. "She was hiding in the boathouse with a paddle in her hands."

Everyone in the room, and those at its door, were listening without scarcely breathing. Then a stocky man in a gray jacket, holding a cap in his hand and with a badge gleaming on his chest, pushed his way in. He was looking a little grim.

"Got the C.B. message but never expected to run into something like this." He looked around at the others and then his glance came back to Carla. "I'll have to book you, Miss." He scratched his chin and looked to be in deep thought. "As I make it out, you and your friend here" — he motioned with his head toward Roger Platt — "knocked the young feller out. Then one of you rowed him out to the deepest part of the lake, took his oars away, and then came back to shore in the other boat."

Amanda remembered then that there had been something strange seen through the mist at the dock. The boats had been missing.

The sheriff said sternly, "Yes, you'll have to come along and be booked, Miss. Your friend, too. I haven't got all the details yet, but it looks like a case of assault, if not attempted homicide."

Carla began to scream, seeming to have lost all her self-control. "It was just a joke, I tell you! I meant to go back and give him the oars but some-one came along in a speedboat just when he was coming out of it."

Amanda could not bear to look at her when she said, "What's going to happen to my share of the money, that's what I want to know!" She began to sound aggrieved. "I will get everything Grandmère left me!"

19.

THE will was finally read. Michael Blake, who was determined to be in the thick of things, called Robert Grace, Roger Platt's associate. The man looked stunned when he learned what had been happening at Chanson du Lac, but his voice scarcely faltered as he read the will, which had been drawn up some years ago.

There was nothing dramatic or astounding about it. Madame had bequeathed the house and all its furnishings to "my good friend and devoted servant, Matilde Gerard." There was a stipulation that it was never to be sold regardless of how attractive the offers of purchase might be. Madame, who had despised the encroaching condominiums, had arranged things so that the estate would never be destroyed to make room for their construction at the lakefront. A trust fund was to be set up for the purpose of maintaining Chason du Lac, and Matilde was to be its trustee.

Glancing at the housekeeper, Amanda saw that she looked as though a million gold coins had fallen into her lap. It was what she had longed for, been afraid to hope for. To live a lonely life in the house that had sheltered her for so long was all that Matilde had wished. When Carla was out of her life, she would doubtlessly be happier.

Amanda was sure that Matilde would not have to go to prison. She was not a criminal. She would not be a menace to anyone now. Surely the authorities would be able to understand that.

The mention in the document of the four young people was brief. Each was to receive twenty thousand dollars, provided it was used as tuition and not for frivolous pursuits. The disposal of the money that would have gone to any persons not present was also set forth. His or her share was to be divided between the others. This had been set forth by Roger Platt. Hearing it again made Amanda even more conscious of its meaning.

"Twenty thousand!" Rick said. "Holy cow! Madame sure was with it. She knew it costs a small fortune to go through college these days. She was a nice old girl at that, wasn't she?"

They were in the back parlor passing the time, for there would not be a bus going in their direction until nine o'clock; Rick had raided the refrigerator and made them all sandwiches. Matilde had protested, but he had refused to let her do anything, telling her teasingly that she was a rich heiress and that preparing meals was below the dignity of someone in her social class.

Ellen kept going to the mirror over the fireplace

and talking silently into it. She was trying to see how she looked when she spoke. Rick was about to say something, but Amanda shook her head. "It's been such a long time. Let her enjoy it."

He was silent for a little while and then curiosity and impatience got the better of him and he said, "Come on now, we've waited long enough. We've pampered you because we thought you might be too upset to talk about it. Give, girl!"

She asked, "What do you want to know?"

He replied, "All of it."

She drew a long breath. "You know the important part already. Carla wanted all the money from her grandmother's estate. If the rest of us weren't there at the time of the reading, she'd have accomplished that. Provided, of course, that she was there herself. You remember hearing the clause about how anyone who was confined to prison or to a mental institution was disqualified. So that was it. She planned to keep Rick and me from getting to the music room in time, and you, Mandy, were to have been certified as insane."

Amanda felt herself shivering. "Those things she did. Pretending to be Madame and coming into my room at night. It was easy to put that over. She did resemble her grandmother, and in her clothes and with the light so bad . . . Well, of course Carla was always good at play-acting."

"She was in the tower room making sounds like crying," Rick put in. "We saw the footprints in there, two sets of them. So there must have been a point when Matilde was helping her."

The spirits of all them sank a little with that thought. Poor Matilde, Amanda thought. With her devotion to the granddaughter of her adored mistress, she had allowed herself to be drawn into something that must have been repugnant to her true nature.

They cheered up a little when Rick said, "But someone saved you when you would have fallen downstairs, Mandy. I wonder if that will all come out when they hold the hearing for true cause."

The two girls looked blank. Matilde had not been arrested. Whether she would be depended upon Carla, who was perhaps at this moment being questioned. Or upon Roger Platt, that weak man who had evidently been in love with Carla since she was a child, and who had been too eager to fall in with her evil schemes.

Ellen said, "I heard a great deal that I wasn't supposed to hear. When you cannot speak, some people think you are deaf, too. And there are places to hide — a great many of them — in this house. Yes, I heard what went on between Carla and Matilde, but one time I was caught. It was at the time Carla put that piece of twine across the steps. She was promising Matilde that you would not be hurt, only frightened. It would strengthen her case, she said, when the time came to question Mandy's sanity. That's what it was all about. I knew but I could not tell. Carla said she would kill me if I did, and I thought she might."

There was more. Rick and Amanda waited and finally Ellen went on speaking. "So I could not tell you. I was afraid she would somehow find out if I wrote anything down. So I tried to send you messages in a different way."

Rick and Amanda looked at her without speaking, and she said impatiently, "The music. I thought you would get the idea from the song titles. I put them where you would be sure to see them, the ones with 'home' in them. 'Home on the Range' and 'Home, Sweet Home.' And there were the others like 'Come Back to Erin,' and you should have guessed that it all meant that Carla had come back home."

Rick and Amanda exchanged glances and then burst out laughing. When she was sober again Amanda asked, "But where did Charlene come in? You left that for us to see, didn't you?"

Ellen looked a little shame-faced. "That was pretty far out, I will admit. But I was getting nowhere with the music. You didn't even come close. Well, Carla is the feminine of Carl — and Carl and Charles are the same name in several languages. And Charlene is the feminine — "

"Of Charles." Rick groaned. "You sure were reaching, honey. It sounds like algebra, which was always my worst subject."

But he got up and crossed the room, put his arms around her, and hugged her. "Never mind, sweetie, you can't win 'em all. I guess we've got the whole story now."

"Not quite," Amanda protested. "A couple of more things. All right, the perfume bit isn't important. It was simply that Carla must have dropped a bottle of it when she was changing clothes in Madame's bedroom. But there was something a lot worse. I was pushed into the cellar. There was water somewhere, and I might have, might have . . . drowned in that dark and dreadful place."

She put her face in her hands, remembering. Ellen said consolingly, "Carla shut off the main pipe for a few minutes, and then when she turned it on again it made a rushing sound. She found me in the kitchen fixing the electrical switch that controls the cellar lights, and she was so furious I thought she would kill me then and there. I ran and hid in the boathouse but she found me there. She dragged me over to the edge of the dock and — well, you know the rest now."

"She must have forgotten everything — the will, Amanda here, me out in the middle of the lake — in her burst of temper," Rick said softly. "She always was like that, you know. This is all typically Carla — the selfishness, the rage when things didn't go just her way."

Amanda turned to look at him with eyes that were beginning to glow with a bright light.

"But I thought that you and she — "

"Not that." He was wearing a broad grin. "More like thee and me." He became serious again, "That was kid stuff, what was between Carla and me. I got over it a long time ago, only a little while after our last visit here."

They were staring into each other's eyes with such absorption that they were startled when Ellen said, "You don't want to hear the rest? I thought you couldn't wait."

"The music!" Amanda cried, remembering. "Where did the music come from when the room was empty?"

Ellen asked with aggravating slowness, "Have you ever heard of an aeolian harp?" When they shook their heads, she explained. "It's something like an autoharp, in shape and size, that is. It's the only instrument I know of that plays without hands. If you put it in front of an open window, the wind comes through it and makes a mournful sort of music. Madame picked it up in Europe some years ago, it seems. Carla knew about it, and Matilde did, too. They thought it would be a good way of confusing you, Amanda. That's what you heard in the middle of the night. I was hoping you'd find out the truth, because I knew what Carla would do to me if I told. And she nearly did," she said simply.

She stood up and Amanda asked, "Where are you going now?"

"I thought I'd get my things together. You know, pack up my belongings."

"But you're all packed," Amanda protested. "I helped you, remember? As a matter of fact, your bag is out there by the door."

There was a secret smile on Ellen's lips as she left the room. Amanda, feeling bewildered, turned to Rick. "He didn't mention why we were brought down here five days early, but I suppose they had to have time to play their tricks and try to prove that I was — I was . . . What's that word? Oh, yes, incompetent. I was going to tell Ellen about Matilde using that little bit of slang, but I'm sure she can figure it out. She learned it from Carla, of course. But why did Ellen go off and leave us alone here? Oh!" she cried as a light seemed to flash somewhere in her brain.

"Yes," he said " 'Oh!' is right. She's a smart

kid, my sister. She knows when a couple of people would like to be alone."

He crossed to where she was standing. He picked up her hand and held it for a moment or two. Then he said urgently, "After all I've been through, I think I deserve more than a hand to hold."

She laughed and said, "Poor you!" Then there was no more time for words. He kissed her, a tender, satisfactory kiss, and it seemed at that moment that the shadows lurking in the big, old house lifted, and she knew that never again would she feel the weight upon her spirit.